*For my daughters*
*Jenny and Kate*


✛ ✛ ✛


DISCARD

*Works of art are of an infinite solitariness . . . only love can apprehend and hold them, and can be just toward them.*

✢ Ranier Maria Rilke

✛✛✛✛✛✛✛✛✛✛✛✛✛✛✛✛✛✛✛✛✛✛✛✛✛✛✛✛✛✛

# PROLOGUE

✛✛✛✛✛✛✛✛✛✛✛✛✛✛✛✛✛✛✛✛✛✛✛✛✛✛✛✛✛✛

EFORE ME, the paintings my father made for Mijnheer van Ruijven: the world I once knew. "Extraordinarily, vigorously, and delightfully painted," according to the auction catalogue. There are twenty-one of them, and Father has been dead now twenty-one years. They have fared better than we children at staying together without him. There were eleven of us when he died, and all of us have gone our separate ways.

But that is another story. I have not come here to mourn the loss of my family. Nor have I come to mourn the loss of that earlier time, only to see it once more in the paintings my father made of it. And here they are, full of light. The auction house is full, the mood expectant. Who will leave with the most desirable of them when the day is through? Who will settle for the girl I once was?

Let me explain. I am not the beautiful daughter. Not Maria, there on the easel, the one who looks over her shoulder at you, caught turning for one last glance before disappearing into the darkness behind her. I am Carelina, the plain girl in the portrait that hangs beside her. Dull brown hair, thin lips. Even my gray-blue robe is dull, the color of a dove. My sister is color and motion and promise. I am pale, as if lit by moonlight, and still. Then and now, all I know, all I am remains inside me.

Only once, briefly, did I wish to be Maria. I do not wish to be Maria now. Nonetheless, when I hear whispering beside me, I bow my head and pray not to be recognized.

"Ah, the girl with the pearl earring!"

"Exquisite."

"They say it is his daughter."

"Yes. And the little plain one, too—another daughter."

They grow quiet then, pitying me I suppose.

It is all right, I tell them silently. I know that the portrait my father painted of me is nowhere near as pleasing as the one he painted of my sister. You would not be alone if you did not understand why he wanted to paint me at all. Upon glancing into the painting room to see Father arranging the gray robe on my shoulders, my own grandmother had stopped and asked why he did not paint, instead, a picture he might hope to sell.

"Come, Mother Thins," he said. "Look at your granddaughter. Do you not see the light inside her?"

But she remained in the doorway, scowling. "I do not have time for looking at light, Johannes," she said. "I must use the light. That is what the day is for: working." And she turned away, into the dark corridor.

Father smiled at me. "God help her," he said. "She does not understand."

The whisperers probably would not understand either. One looks at my father's paintings and either sees what he saw, sees why he had no choice but to follow his heart; or one does not see. It is true that if he had been a more sensible man he would have painted many more pictures, the kind that fetched hundreds of guilders. It is true, too, that sometimes I wonder how different our lives would have been if he had done so and thus freed himself, freed all of us from Grandmother's dark, joyless home. He might have grown old and wise. I might be with him yet, mixing his paints, making his brushes, helping him to arrange those same loved objects to catch the light in ways that were ever new.

But looking at the glorious pictures before me, I think—to earn so many guilders he would have had to paint differently. And that I do not care to imagine. Nor do I care to imagine any life I might have led, no matter how comfortable, if it did not have in it this portrait that my father made of me. There is nothing I would trade for the memory that looking at it brings: his eyes upon me, his hands at work, claiming me particle by particle for the canvas.

Suddenly, he is present, fluttering through me. As true and elusive as the girl in the portrait. The girl I was.

I should go now, I think. I stand to go. I had only wanted to see my father's pictures one last time, to steal a few moments to honor him. Now I have done so. But I am made weak by their light. It pours into me. I vibrate with their color.

"Are you ill, Vrouw?" the whisperer asks.

"No, no," I say. "Please. Do not trouble yourself about me."

But gently he places his hands on my shoulders, lowers me to my chair. He does not make a fuss. With the palm of his hand, he says, "Stay." And I do. I am grateful for the wine he brings, grateful that he nods kindly at my thanks and then, as the auctioneer raises his gavel, leaves me to drink it alone. To remember.

# VIEW OF DELFT

Y SISTERS were fast asleep all round me—Maria, Elisabeth, Cornelia, Beatrix, Aleydis. But I woke, crossed by a slice of light sneaking in through the worn green curtains of our sleeping cupboard, and I could not stay abed. I whispered a waking prayer, climbed out, and slipped on my clothes. Then, tying my cap under my chin, I climbed the steep narrow stairway, tiptoeing past the room where Grandmother slept, to the big room at the corner of the house where Father made his paintings. He was always there at first light, preparing his materials before he settled at his easel to paint. But this morning when I peeked in, I saw only the sun pouring through the open window. It made a path across the table, touching the objects that Father had arranged there—a wooden box, a string of pearls, a folded sheet of paper—and making them shine. There was no one there at all, except for the woman in the painting that Father had left on the easel. In time, she would become our mother, I knew. But this morning, she was still faceless: any woman standing before a window, reading a letter.

Downstairs in the cooking kitchen, Tanneke was kneading dough on the big wood table. She put a floury finger to her lips to let me know that Mother and Gretje, the baby, were still sleeping in the next room.

"Father?" I whispered.

She smiled and glanced toward the door, then returned to her kneading. I waited till she began to hum; then I drifted away, quiet as smoke, through the house and out into the morning, where I caught just a glimpse of my father striding along the Oude Langendijk Canal before he turned the corner and disappeared down Koornmarkt Street. His legs were so long and carried him so quickly wherever he wanted to go that I should never have hoped to catch him, but for what I knew: sooner or later, something would strike him and he would be compelled to stop a while and look at it.

I knew, too, that I should not set out alone to follow him. Grandmother had told us story after story about children falling into the canals and drowning, run over by sledges, trampled by horses. Girls spirited away by peddlers and left to beg in the streets. There were so many ways a young one could be lost. But just as I could not stay abed once the light had touched me, I could not keep from running into the light now.

Soon Father came into my view. He stood very still in the shadow of a linden tree, his head cocked to better observe whatever had caught his attention. I stopped and looked, too, wondering what it was that had pleased him. I saw lacy patterns of light on the cobblestones, tree trunks black and shining from last night's rain. I raised my eyes to the very top of the Oude Kerk and saw the black-faced clock with its gold numerals, its red lions and gilded town crest. Four turrets, sturdy as soldiers, lifted the spire of the church right into the sky. That's where heaven was. God lived there, among the clouds; but I did not look for Him, for Grandmother had told me that He could not be seen by the likes of us. Only by the angels.

Father began to walk again, and I hurried after him. Past the orphanage with its two stone children above the door, past the East India Company that smelled of faraway lands, to the place where all the canals came together and made a little harbor. Housemaids, like our Tanneke, stood on the sandy quay, their shopping pails hooked over their arms, waiting for the fishermen to bring in their catch. Gulls waited, too, swooping and squawking. There was a transport boat, with a long red cabin where the travelers sat. I should like to live on such a boat, I thought, rocked by the gentle waves on the harbor, always pulling in the anchor and heading off to some new town. All of us: Father, Mother, and my sisters. Not Grandmother Thins, though, for she would not approve of living that way.

Father stopped at the bridge that would take him across the harbor and looked back toward the town. I stepped behind a tree, but not before he saw me.

"Ah, Carelina," he called. "Come. Do not hide from your own father." He stooped and opened his arms, and I went to him, breathed him in. His woolen doublet. Tobacco, sunshine, the piney smell of Venice turpentine. He put his big hands on my shoulders and stood, looking down at me.

"I should scold you for following me," he said.

But he did not scold me; nor did he tell me that I must go back. He smiled at me and took my hand. "I will show you something," he said. "It will be our secret.

We walked on, across the bridge to a house with green shutters. Father stopped in front of it and waved his hand toward the harbor. "Look," he said, and I saw the Rotterdam Gate with its two blue turrets, our whole town of Delft behind it, shining in the morning sun. Father knocked on the door then, and a man opened it. He nodded, nothing more; and Father and I walked past him, through the front hall and up the stairs. At the landing, there were three closed doors. He stopped before one of them and knelt down beside me.

"It is a kind of magic, what you will see inside," he said. "Do not be afraid."

I was never afraid when I was with him. Still, when we entered the room and he closed the door behind us, I trembled to see our

11

town of Delft again, this time floating before me in utter darkness. The water in the harbor sparkled. Dots of light were strung across a blue herring boat near the Rotterdam Gate and along the rooftops, like little pearls. In the distance, the spire of the Nieuwe Kerk was so bright that it seemed to have been touched by the hand of God.

Father raised my hand toward the Rotterdam Gate, and I hesitated before touching it, fearing that my fingers would go right through, just as they would if I touched a ghost. But they did not go through. Nor did my fingers feel the brick that I knew the real gate was made of. They felt the slick surface of linen, prepared as I knew Father prepared it to take paint.

This surprised me so much that I laughed in delight. Father laughed, too. He opened the door of the room, threw open a shutter, and the town disappeared, leaving nothing but a big blank canvas hung upon a wall. He showed me how all the windows had been fitted with wood shutters that were painted black, in order to keep out every bit of light; how a small, round hole had been drilled into one that faced the harbor, and fitted with two lenses. These lenses, he said, had been made by his friend, Mijnheer van Leeuwenhoek, to capture the town in a beam of light and carry it onto the canvas.

"You remember my *camera obscura*, Carelina," he went on.

I nodded. This, Mijnheer van Leeuwenhoek, a scientist, had made as well. It was a wooden box fitted with a lens, and if you looked into the square of glass set into the top of it, you saw a tiny picture of whatever had been placed before the lens. Father used it in his painting room to help him decide what a picture would be.

"Is it the same then?" I asked. "Only so much larger?"

"Yes." He looked surprised and pleased that I had understood this.

"And will you paint the picture on the wall for Mijnheer van Ruijven?"

I hoped he would. If so, I might be able to go to Mijnheer van Ruijven's house with him when the painting was hung and visit with Magdalena, Mijnheer van Ruijven's daughter. In her sleeping room, she had a house for her dolls, a *poppenhuis*, and if I was nice to her, and very careful, she allowed me to arrange and rearrange the tiny china dishes and the brass candlesticks, to move the dolls from their chairs by the fireplace to their tiny curtained beds.

"Yes," Father said. "I will paint the picture for Mijnheer Van Ruijven. But it will take a few months' time."

He closed the door and the shutters again, and the town re-appeared. He went and stood before the place where I now knew the canvas was, so that the prow of the blue boat seemed to be painted on his face. With a piece of chalk that he took from his pocket, he followed the line of the quay, the boats in the harbor, the town wall, the Scheidam and Rotterdam Gates, the spires and rooftops behind them, the clouds above. At times, as he worked, some part of the town was cast onto his back or arm or head, and he would have to bend his body awkwardly so that the image appeared on the canvas, where it belonged, and he could outline it.

I watched. I did not know how much time had passed when he stepped away from the town and disappeared into the darkness. Only the sound of his voice let me know that he was near. "Enough for this morning," he said. "My stomach is rumbling. Shall we go home now, and eat?"

Suddenly, I thought of Mother and Grandmother, who were surely well awake by now and gone to mass without me. No doubt I would soon get the scolding I knew full well I should have gotten from my father. But I could not be sorry that I followed him and saw what I saw. Everything in the world looked different because of it. And new. Along Achterom, where it was dark and narrow, I saw for the first time how the lily pads crowded against the slick mossy walls of the canal. Where it turned and the water was struck by sunlight, the tangled strands of grasses floating just below the surface looked like long, green hair.

"Father, may I come with you tomorrow?" I asked. "Please? May I come every morning and watch until the painting is all through?"

He spoke gently. "I cannot think you truly want that, Carelina. Nothing to do but sit and watch me paint."

"But I always watch you," I said. "When Mother and Grandmother think I'm playing, I creep into your painting room. I am so quiet you do not know I'm there."

He stopped then and looked at me in a way he had never looked at me before, the way he looked at whatever he was painting. "All right then," he said after a long moment. "You may come. If you don't mind getting up at first light. If you will sit quietly all the while I work and not disturb me."

"Yes," I said. "Yes, I promise."

He was quiet the rest of our walk. He didn't seem to notice anything. Not me, walking beside him. Not the shopkeepers just beginning to stir along Brabantse, or the slice of Great Markt Square that came into view. He was painting in his head, I knew, seeing the town floating before him, even as we were walking through it toward home.

✢ ✢ ✢ ✢ ✢

Grandmother's house was in *Papenhoek*, where only Catholics lived. Beside it was the secret church. It was made of two houses, connected in the attic, where the faithful gathered to hear the Jesuit brothers say mass. To be Catholic was not allowed in our land. We must not speak of our faith, except among ourselves, and so our Catholic neighbors were especially dear to us. Now, as Father and I turned onto Oude Langendyjk, these neighbors woke him from his reverie, bidding him good morning. Mijnheer Samuels, the stone mason, bade him come later and see what progress he had made on a statue of the Holy Mother the Jesuits had commissioned. Mevrouw Huybrechts, the bookseller, called out to tell him of a folio received from Amsterdam the day before that he would surely want to examine. Mijnheer de Cocq, the apothecary, hailed him from inside his shop, where he sat in his black robe and pointed hat, beneath a stuffed crocodile—the sign of his guild.

Father paused before the open doorway. "Come, Carelina," he said, and I gladly followed him inside.

It was smoky there. The scent of tobacco swirled up from Mijnheer de Cocq's clay pipe and mingled with a dozen other scents: roots and herbs he prescribed to cure the townfolk of anything that ailed them, musky red wine in wooden casks, oils, turpentine. And cats. He kept them to chase the mice out of his cupboards.

He closed the big book of remedies that he had been reading, pushed his silver spectacles down onto the tip of his nose, and looked at me over the lenses. "Why, it is Carelina," he said. "The beautiful daughter."

Of course, this was not true. Everyone in Papists' Corner knew that my sister Maria was the beauty among us; but I was the daughter Mijnheer de Cocq liked best, and so I smiled at him, knowing I was indeed beautiful in his eyes.

"I am commissioned by van Ruijven to paint a view of the city," Father told him. "It is to be quite large."

Mijnheer de Cocq turned to the big wood cupboard where he kept the pigments, each rich pure powder in its own tiny drawer. Yellow ocher, madder lake, umber. These were earth pigments, I knew, for Father had told me. The umber and ocher were made from the very earth itself; the madder lake from the red roots of a plant. And then ultramarine, the most dear. It was made from the lapis lazuli stone, the color of the Virgin Mary's robe. Grandmother had a rosary made of these stones. I tried not to envy my sister Elisabeth, the most devout of us children, when Grandmother allowed her to pray with it, sternly reminding myself that touching the beautiful blue beads could not bring me any closer to God than would touching the amber beads of my own, poorer rosary. Still, I longed to slide the blue beads through my fingers.

Mijnheer de Cocq listened carefully to Father's instructions, writing the name of each pigment and the amount needed. He would weigh them on his brass scales and wrap them in paper. He would measure nut oil and Venice turpentine into little flasks, and prepare the hog bristle and sable from which Father would make his brushes. This afternoon, his apprentice would deliver everything to Father's new painting room above the harbor.

Father always bought the finest supplies, and sometimes it was necessary to ask Mijnheer de Cocq to do him the favor of allowing credit until he had the means to pay. Today, though, his leather purse was full of guilders that Mijnheer van Ruijven had given him. Happily, he counted out the correct number of coins and bade Mijnheer de Cocq good morning. We walked on then, past the Jesuit School and the church to Grandmother's house, which stood at the point where Oude Langendijck and the Molenpoort came together.

Inside, it smelled of bread baking. Father went to his painting room to think; and I went to the kitchen, where Tanneke was just taking the *broodjes* from the oven. They were brown and crackly on top, glazed with her special mix of butter and eggs.

She smiled when she looked up and saw me, but then a ripple of worry crossed her face. "The others have gone to mass," she said. "Even the baby. Grandmother was not happy to find you missing."

"I was with Father," I said.

"Yes." Tanneke put her hand on my shoulder. "I knew this, and told her. But, Carelina, you must not sneak away like that again. If I had not followed you to the door and seen you set off after your father, I should have been frightened when I realized you were gone— and, soon enough, in trouble with your grandmother for not having kept watch over you."

I hung my head. I did not ever want to frighten Tanneke, or cause Grandmother's wrath to fall upon her. I adored her. When she was baking, she sneaked me raisins and dates that should have gone into the bread. If I sat at the big wooden table and kneaded the dough for her, she told me what she knew. You should put a dog into bed with a sick child, she said, for the dog will take in the child's ailment. At night, you should lay your stockings in a cross at the foot of your bed to ward off evil spirits.

Grandmother always said, "Don't listen to her. She is foolish." But I listened anyway.

Once, I hid outside the painting room and listened to her talk to Father all the while he painted her. He should take care when traveling by stagecoach, she told him. If anyone had dyed or false hair, he should get off immediately and wait for the next coach, because that meant highwaymen would attack. She knew it was so, she said. Her brother had told her.

Father laughed. Tanneke was standing in the corner of his painting room, near the leaded window. She was wearing her red skirt and her yellow chamois jacket; its green sleeves with their violet cuffs pushed up above her elbows. Her white kerchief was folded back to show her high forehead; a blue apron was wrapped around her waist. Father had covered the little square table before her with a green cloth, then rumpled a blue cloth exactly the color of her apron and let it drape down over the green. He had set three *broodjes* in one corner, a blue jug in another, and a brown bowl between them. Taking up most of the rest of the table was a basket with a round loaf of bread in it. The gray wall behind her he left blank, but for the line of blue and white tiles at the base. A square market basket, a little mirror, and a copper pail hung from nails on the narrow strip of wall beside the window.

He handed her an earthen pitcher. She tilted it, brought her free hand to support it from below, and a cool white ribbon of milk poured into the bowl on the table.

"Yes," he said. "Again, please."

Over and over, Tanneke poured the milk from the pitcher into the bowl, until Father captured it in paint. Weeks later, when the little picture was finished, he took it to Mijnheer van Ruijven's home, where it was hung in the kitchen. When Tanneke carried something from our house to theirs, a gift of bread or sweets to thank Mijnheer van Ruijven for some kindness, she refused to look at it. It was too much like her, she said. If she looked, her living spirit would be drawn right into it.

Would she be frightened if Father and I took her to see the town floating in the dark room, I wondered? Probably so. In any case, I dared not tell her or anyone else what I had seen. Grandmother would not like the idea of such magic, I knew. She would think it was the work of the devil. And Mother would not like the idea of my following Father there. She liked to have him for herself. If I told my sisters, they would want to see it, too. But it was my secret with Father. He had said so. Tomorrow, only I would return there with him.

Knowing I would have this pleasure made me want to be good. Cheerfully, I went to the cellar for Tanneke to bring up the butter and cheese. The cheese was round, like a wheel, covered with red wax, which I peeled back so that I could slice it with a sharp knife. Cheese and warm *broodjes* with butter. A cup of milk. It made my mouth water to anticipate the meal.

I arranged the herring on a plate, then began to peel and slice the apples Tanneke had set before me. Soon I heard the clatter of footsteps and then the voices of my sisters and of our mother and grandmother.

"Well," Grandmother said, at the sight of me.

It was all she said, but that one word carried with it volumes of displeasure. I kept my head bowed to the task Tanneke had given me. It was not Grandmother I avoided looking at, but our mother. I could not bear to see the anxiety my absence had likely caused her, for I knew I could not bring myself to regret it.

Grandmother did not scold me. Worse, she spoke about my failures to our mother, and I must listen or rudely leave the room. I was a willful girl, she said. Of all her grandchildren, I was the one who could least afford to shirk the daily ritual and guidance of our faith. Of all of us, she feared most for my immortal soul.

My face burned with anger and humiliation. While I might be willful at times, I was far less willful than her beloved Maria. She would have a thing if she wanted it, be it a bit of lace for a new dress, or Cornelia's music book, or our mother's complete attention. She was often mean as well, pinching Aleydis and Cornelia when no one was looking, or kicking me under the table with her sharp wooden clogs. I was never knowingly unkind. Mother knew this, yet she failed to speak in my defense, only murmured a kind of vague concern and then slipped away with the baby, Gretje, to the front room.

Nor did I argue my own merits. I dared not; for to argue with Grandmother would surely bring some punishment upon me. But I could not bring myself to confess any wrong and bent stubbornly over the bowl of apples until I heard I the jangle of her household keys and then her footsteps as she ascended the front stairs to prepare herself for the morning meal.

Maria, the oldest of us, laughed when Grandmother was out of earshot. Then she grabbed her skipping rope and swished by, bumping me—purposely, I was certain—on her way to the back garden.

Elisabeth, wearing a disapproving expression, followed with Beatrix and Aleydis in tow. Only Cornelia remained near me.

"You were with our father," she whispered. "Grandmother knew this before we left for mass because Tanneke told her. I can see no reason for her to be so angry."

I shrugged, as if it were no matter to me. "She does not love me," I said. But speaking the words brought tears to my eyes, and I must wipe them away with the back of my hand.

Tears came to my sister's eyes as well. "Oh, Carelina," she said. "No. You cannot think—"

"You know it is so," I interrupted. "She could not love me, or she would not treat me as she does. But it does not hurt me as badly as you think, Cornelia, for I do not love her either. I cannot. Indeed, why *you* love her, I cannot imagine. You make every effort to please her, yet she treats you nearly as badly as she treats me. She loves Maria because she is beautiful. And Elisabeth—her little nun. The rest of us . . ."

I stopped then, for I looked up and saw Cornelia's shocked expression.

What I had said was true. Grandmother doted on Maria and Elisabeth, favored them in all things; the rest of us she seemed to regard as a burden. My plain looks and stubborn ways were a particular trial to her. Indeed, I had so resisted her efforts to make a young lady of me that she had lately withdrawn me from Mejuffrouw van Aeckel's Jesuit School for Girls and put me in the care of Tanneke, whom she bade to teach me the best she could, so that I might be prepared to manage a household should some foolish young man ever condescend to marry me someday. I did not miss the afternoons spent among my sisters and their friends learning fine needlework and deportment. I had ruined countless linen embroidery cloths, stretching the thread too tightly or spotting them with my pricked fingers.

Practicing proper conversation, I could not think of a thing to say. Nonetheless, I resented Grandmother all the more for giving up on me completely. This, I knew, was not fair of me. Nor was it fair to draw Cornelia into my quarrels with her, especially knowing that Cornelia's loyalty to me so often gave Grandmother license to find fault with her.

"I am sorry," I said. "I was wrong to speak of Grandmother harshly. Please. I beg your forgiveness."

This she gave me without hesitation, wrapping her arms around me in a fierce embrace. When we gathered to eat—Grandmother at the head of the table; Mother, Father, Tanneke, and my sisters and I along the sides; and Gretje, like the queen of babies in her special chair that looked like a little throne—I bowed my head and prayed to our Lord that I might learn to be more like my sister Cornelia. I ate quietly. I did not beg Father to allow me to accompany him to visit our Grandma Digna that afternoon, as I knew he would—to tell her of his plans for the new painting—even though I dearly loved to visit her. When the meal was finished, I went directly to my knitting basket and took out one of the wool stockings I was making for winter. Grandmother required twenty rows daily; and for once, I knitted them patiently, without complaint.

✛ ✛ ✛ ✛ ✛

The next morning, I woke before first light and lay in the sleeping cupboard perfectly still. The darkness surrounding me, black as velvet, brought back the dark room with the city floating in it, and I wondered how Father would be able to paint if he could not see to mix the colors on his palette. Surely, he has thought of this, I told myself. I tried not to listen to Grandmother's voice in my head, saying with a sigh how impractical Father was. How, if he weren't so stubborn, he would paint the portraits of rich burghers instead of laboring for weeks and months at a time on such odd subjects as lazy, sleeping girls and housemaids pouring milk.

Even this picture that Mijnheer van Ruijven had commissioned annoyed her. Father did not ask enough for his services, I had heard her tell Mother just last night, after he had given us our lessons and gone upstairs to his painting room. She complained, too, about the supplies he had bought from Mijnheer de Cocq. Why must he always use the most expensive pigments and oils? How would Mijnheer Van Ruijven know the difference?

I made myself remember how Father just smiled and gazed at her kindly when she fretted. "She is good to us," was all he said if any of us complained of her ill temper. Still, I feared what she would say if she found out about Mijnheer Van Leeuwenhoek's lenses. Guilders spent on the devil! And the devil aside, I knew she'd wonder as I did how Father meant to paint in the dark.

I did not want, ever, to think anything that Grandmother thought—especially about my father. So I turned my thoughts elsewhere, willed the bed curtains to fade from black to gray with the beginning of daylight.

Dressing, I heard Tanneke's step on the cellar stairs. She entered the kitchen, rubbing the sleep from her eyes. She handed me some bread and cheese wrapped in a cloth. "So you and Father won't go hungry," she said. "Yes, I know where you are going. He has told me."

"Grandmother . . . ?" I said.

Tanneke's eyes were merry. "He has announced his intention," she said. " 'I shall claim one daughter,' he told her. 'And you may rest assured that, while she is with me, I shall keep her hands busy and keep watch on her immortal soul.' "

Father had claimed me? I felt myself flush with pleasure.

Tanneke saw this and smiled. "Go now," she said, with a little push to my shoulders. "Listen, the floor is creaking in the front room with his footsteps. He is ready."

I took our breakfast and met him at the door. He did not speak, just brushed the bottom of my chin with his fingertips and nodded approvingly, as if I had passed some kind of test. We went out into the street, where the buildings and trees and statues were still no more than dark shapes against the lightening sky, the cobblestones like rough pewter. The moon floated in the dark water of the canal. As we walked, the world took on color. Roofs and bricks and shutters became red, leaves green. The moon disappeared, leaving the sky blue, except for one gray cloud floating in from the sea.

I glanced at Father walking beside me and saw that his fingers were moving slowly—stretching, flexing—as if dreaming of the brush. I did not speak, for I could see that what he wanted at this moment was my silence.

Finally, approaching the house on the harbor, he remembered I was with him. "So, Carelina," he said, "we begin."

I could do no more than whisper, "Yes."

The upstairs room, with all the shutters open, was filled with light. The pigments and supplies that Father had bought from Mijnheer de Cocq the day before were set on a long wood table— the only furniture in the room besides a three-cornered stool that he would sit on sometimes to paint. Also on the table, there was a marble slab and, on it, a stone muller for grinding the pigments. There were little pots to mix the paint in. Brushes, palettes, a palette knife. The mahlstick with its ivory knob on one end that Father sometimes rested against the canvas and leaned his painting hand on to keep it steady.

Now he stood a long time looking out the window that framed the harbor. I stood beside him and tried to see what he saw. It seemed to me more or less the same as what I had seen the day before: boats in the harbor, women with market baskets on the quay, the morning sun shining on the tower of the Nieuwe Kerk in the distance. But when Father closed the shutters, and I turned to look at the town floating on the canvas, I saw that it was not exactly the same as the real town had been. Some colors were richer and deeper, as if they were wet. Some objects were fuzzy at the edges. They looked the way chimneys and tree-tops looked when they were back-lit by the sun. Bits of light gathered and sparkled so brightly on the water and along the hull of the blue herring boat that they hurt my eyes.

I wondered again how Father would be able to paint what was before him when everything in the room but the floating town was dark. Then, without speaking, he answered my question. He looked a long time at the town on the canvas, then opened all the shutters and let the light in again. Yesterday he had prepared the lead white pigment; now he ground it with nut oil and turpentine, used the knife to smear the finished paint onto his palette. He laid in the quay in the bottom corner of the canvas, then the light parts of the water and a vast sky that would be more than half of the picture when it was through. The shape of the town that he had outlined yesterday with chalk was left blank—narrow and ragged between the water and the sky.

Though he often looked out the window at the real town, he did not paint exactly what he saw. Nor did he paint the town exactly as the lens made it appear. He painted a city he saw in his mind. He changed it, too, so that as the summer days passed, the town that emerged beneath his brush was and was not the same town that we walked through at the end of every morning, returning to Grandmother's house, where Tanneke prepared the midday meal.

Father taught me to clean his brushes, soaking the bristles in turpentine just long enough to loosen the paint, then washing them in soap and water, taking care to stroke the bristles as I would stroke the fur of a cat—gently, in the right direction, and rinsing them with clean water until the suds bore no trace of color. I must clean the metal collar that held the handle and bristles together, as well, and wipe the grinding slab with a rag soaked in solvent, for Father did not like to see an errant spot of paint anywhere when he closed the door upon his morning's work. When I had proven myself patient enough to accomplish these tasks to his satisfaction, he taught me how to grind his colors.

Often, he held forth on the properties of pigments, describing each one with such enthusiasm, making its history and character, its quirky and unpredictable behaviors seem as fascinating as those of a living person. Comfortable, ancient ochres, born of the earth—as similar and opposite as members of a family, he said—some valued for their excellent hiding power, others for their transparency. Hard, haughty lapis lazuli first brought by caravan across the Orient. Sharp edged, like a beautiful blue splinter; yet oddly fragile, too, for lapis must be worked up with great care, else it would lose the exquisite violet tone which most recommended it.

He displayed coarse grounds of the pigment in his open palm as he spoke, then brushed them from his hand to the slab. He added nut oil drop by drop, and showed me how to use a blunt palette knife to rub the mixture into a stiff paste, taking care to gather the paste into a small area of the slab and to work it no more than was needed to make it smooth and uniform. Then, using a slight but steady pressure, he rubbed it in a back-and-forth, somewhat circular motion with a glass muller to assure that as much of the paste as possible was ground over with each complete rub. He showed me how to gather the paint by scraping it from the sides and bottom of the muller as well as from the slab, and bade me do this frequently, especially at the beginning of the grind.

I was happy at the tasks my father gave me, not only because it pleased me to be of help to him; but, away from Grandmother's critical eye, I felt calm and capable, a worthy person in my own right. Away from the constant reproach of Maria's beauty and Elisabeth's piety, my plain looks did not trouble me; my stubborn, questing spirit found some rest. Mornings sped by. Walking home, I dawdled, pointing out this and that to Father, hoping to capture his attention even if only for a moment, grateful for each delay.

I was always happy to see Cornelia, though. She often waited with one or another of the little ones near Grandmother's doorstep, and I could tell by her expression how the morning had gone. Now she hurried anxiously toward us. Had she come to inform me of some unwitting offense? Bleakness settled inside me at the thought, and I girded myself for a spate of Grandmother's ill temper; but, in fact, her news was worse than what I had imagined. There was to be a singing party at the home of Clementia van der Velde, and I had been invited.

Of course, Maria and Elisabeth were to go, as well. According to Cornelia, it was all they had spoken of since the invitation had arrived by messenger an hour before. Indeed, the chattering continued all through the mid-day meal. Not even Maria had been invited to such a party before, and she and Elisabeth speculated about what the evening would bring. There would be boys from the Jesuit School present, well-mannered, my sisters hoped. Maria had been given a songbook by one of the older girls at Mevrouw van Aeckel's school, and she drew it from her pocket and teased Elisabeth, trilling phrases of a love song which caused her to blush in mortification. She turned to me then.

"You shall wear my yellow dress, Carelina," she said grandly. "It

26

is quite nice. Grandmother says that I may have a new one."

I shrugged. It did not matter to me what I wore; but Grandmother could not know that this was so, and I was wounded by her thoughtlessness. I would not care, I told myself. I would go to the party, for I must. Mijnheer van der Velde was greatly respected in our parish and an occasional patron of Father, as well; it would be unthinkable to refuse an invitation from his daughter.

The appointed evening arrived all too soon. Maria sighed for lack of a carriage, and was cross with Tanneke, whom Grandmother had bade accompany us. As we neared the van der Velde home, she and Elisabeth hurried ahead to join some friends gathered at the entry. I knew these girls, too. *Papenhoek* was so small that it was impossible not to know everyone who lived there. But they acknowledged me with no more than a nod when I reached them; and when the housemaid opened the door, they entered like a flock of birds, leaving me on the doorstep. The maid gave me a questioning glance.

"Go now, *schaapje*," Tanneke said, touching my shoulder in farewell. And so I did.

Clementia van der Velde was a pleasant girl, unspoiled by her family's wealth and position; and I was grateful for her kind greeting, though it could not put me at ease. "You must enjoy yourself, Carelina," she gaily decreed, gesturing toward the drawing room, where refreshments were set out on a long table and the evening's entertainment was ready to begin.

I spotted a chair at the far edge of the gathering, went directly to it, and sat down, folding my hands upon my lap. My heart pounded, then calmed as time passed and it became clear that no one meant to join me. I grew braver then, glancing about at the fine walnut furnishings, the rich Turkish carpets on the tables, the polished marble floors patterned in black and white. Candles flickered in the brass chandelier.

Above the high mantel, in a carved frame, hung Father's *Christ in the House of Mary and Martha*. It was nothing like the pictures he made now. Larger than *View of Delft*, its three figures were life-sized and glowing with color. There were no marble floors or mullioned windows like the ones in the paintings he made of our mother. No gold, no pearls, no ermine jackets. No elegant furnishings, brass pitchers, or porcelain jugs. Just our Lord, in a wooden chair; Martha, leaning over His shoulder to offer Him bread; a contemplative Mary at His feet.

Father had been commissioned to make this work for Mijnheer van der Velde long ago, and in one of my earliest memories I was in this very room with him soon after it was hung. I remembered the vast fireplace, candlelight flickering on the whitewashed walls, the sound of spirited conversation. I remembered Father's voice among the voices of Mijnheer van der Velde and the Jesuit brothers who had gathered to admire the new work of art. And myself still small enough to sit on Father's lap.

My sense of that small self—alert to every possibility, comfortable in her own skin—was so vivid, so real that, closing my eyes, I was transported back to that time. Opening them again, I could not help but be saddened by the awkward girl I had become and by the sight of the dozen or so boys and girls that I had known since childhood gathered at the harpsichord, imitating the behavior of fashionable young men and women.

This sadness stayed with me in the next days, and also the mixture of relief and mortification that I had felt all evening to be so thoroughly ignored. The knowledge of my fate lay heavy on me. Clementia van der Velde's singing party was but the first of many such parties I must suffer through until, finally deemed an old maid, I would be abandoned, pitied, and left in peace.

Still, I did not wish to be anyone but my true self—Carelina, named for Carel Fabritius, my father's dearest friend, whose wondrous little picture of a goldfinch hung in clear view of Father's easel. A student of the great Rembrandt in Amsterdam, Fabritius was—according to all who had known him—one of the few whose gift might have rivaled his master's. But he had died in a terrible explosion that occurred in our town on the twelfth of October in 1654. The very day of my birth.

Born too early—Mother's womb perhaps too weak to hold me to full term so soon after Maria's birth—I had very nearly died myself; and every year on my birthday, Father remembered the death of his friend and told me that he was grateful to God for sparing me. To have lost both friend and child would have been unbearably sad. Thus, I was named for him. And, secretly, deep in my heart, I believed that I was special for this reason.

My first task each morning was to decant the spirits. I uncorked the flask, then slowly, very carefully poured the turpentine into a fresh flask until the sludge that had settled to the bottom overnight loosened and bits of pigment floated free. I must stop pouring instantly when I saw this, dispose of the tainted turpentine and top the flask with fresh, pure spirits. When I had finished this task, I set to grinding.

Father's muller was large and awkward in my small hands; but I loved how it felt there, smooth and cool. I loved the feel of the color beneath it, the way that, when I had ground so long that my forearms ached, I felt the grains of pigment start to go to paste. Sometimes I glanced up and saw Father watching me work, and I knew that he was pleased. When this happened, I allowed myself to dream that he might teach me to paint someday. I had heard him speak admiringly about his friend, Mijnheer Terborch, who taught his daughter to

become a painter, and I prayed that Father might decide to teach me
the same way.

Of course, I knew that if Father were going to teach anyone,
Grandmother Thins would urge him to take in pupils, boys whose
fathers would pay handsomely for the privilege. Boys who could
prepare Father's canvases, make his paints and brushes, and help to
finish his paintings—as his good friend Mijnheer van Hoogstraaten
had once helped to finish the master, Rembrandt's, paintings when
he was apprenticed to him. Not that Grandmother approved of
Mijnheer van Hoogstraaten. He was clever, she allowed, and had a
good head for business. But he was too worldly for her taste—and
once a Mennonite, as well!

I loved Mijnheer van Hoogstraaten, though. He was full of
thoughts and ideas that he told me about, even though I was a child.
And he had seen so much of the world. Once he had lived in Vienna
and worked for the Emperor Ferdinand. He had traveled to Rome,
too, and studied there. Father was to have traveled with him that time,
but did not go because he fell in love with our mother.

What if he had gone, I wondered sometimes. What if I had never
been born? I crossed myself when such thoughts came, and prayed
to God to forgive me for them, for I feared He might think I was
questioning His will.

Grinding, I tried to think pure thoughts. I made a picture of an
angel in my mind, a beautiful angel with a perfect round halo made
of stars. She hovered, all gold and white, with nothing but blue sky
behind her. But I could not keep her there, for I knew that Mijnheer
van Hoogstraaten was coming, and the picture of the angel kept
giving way to him. He was a round, jolly man, with red cheeks and
wild curly hair. The remembered sound of his booming voice in my
head made me smile.

He had sent word to Father that he would be coming on the

water coach from Dordrecht to see his *View of Delft*. When the bells of the Nieuwe Kerk rang at ten o'clock, Father bade me stop grinding and keep watch from the window. I was to tell him when I saw the boat enter the harbor.

It was busy that morning. The last herring boats had docked, and the women on the quay jostled to examine the catch. Water coaches from Gouda and Amsterdam glided in, pulled by sturdy brown horses, and the boatmen lowered the ramps so that the travelers could hurry off into the town. Other travelers waited for the bell to sound so that they could board one of the boats as it continued its journey. There was shouting, the splash of anchors raised and lowered, the clunk of wooden crates being loaded and unloaded. Dogs barked, carriage wheels clattered on the cobblestones.

Behind me, Father painted a town that was absolutely still. When I turned to look at it, the sounds of the outside world faded, and it was as if I were standing on the quay of the painting, looking across the harbor at a magical town that I had never seen before. The water shone like a mirror. I was half-surprised when I drew closer, looked hard at the surface, and did not see my own face peering back at me. I wondered—if I could enter this painted town, what different kind of Delft might I find?

Father laughed when I told him my thoughts. "You know it is not real, Carelina," he said. "Color against color, no more. What lies beyond the gates is no more than a dream." But he stepped back, brush in hand, and took a long look at the painting himself, perhaps trying to see it through my eyes.

Finally, the boat from Dordrecht pulled into the harbor, and Mijnheer van Hoogstraaten was the first one off when it docked. He waved coming down the ramp, already talking. "Jan!" he called to Father. "Maes sends greetings to you. He would have come himself, were it not for a commission he is pressed to finish. But I am to tell him everything about this wonder you have made. And I have brought something to show you, too." He raised the battered leather bag he was carrying; then, reaching us, set it down to throw his arms around Father. It was funny to see: the two men so different in size. Father bent over him, his long arms wrapping around Mijnheer van Hoogstraaten like a spider.

"And *dochterken*!" Mijnheer Hoogstraaten beamed when he untangled himself from Father and saw me there. Little daughter, he called me. He thumped my head three times, as if I were some fruit or vegetable he was deciding whether or not to buy, then strode off with Father toward the bridge, all the while peppering him with questions. How did Father find exactly the right room to work from? Did Mijnheer van Ruijven rent it for him?

"I have seen such a room before," Mijnheer van Hoogstraaten said. "But never one used to make a picture. It is a splendid idea, Jan. Splendid! Was it van Leeuwenhoek who fit the shutter with a lens? And is there a mirror to right the image on the wall?

He turned to me. "It is as the eye works, *dochterken*." He explained how some years ago the scientist, Kepler, had discovered that the eye painted a picture of the world on itself, made of color and light. "But," he announced, "the picture is received upside-down and reversed. Think of it, Carelina." He waved his hand toward the linden trees along the canal and a boy running there, wielding a stick to drive the hoop that spun before him. "What you are seeing at this very moment is completely backward inside your head! And what rights it, I ask? A tiny mirror there? Gilt, perhaps, like the hand mirror on a lady's table." Mijnheer van Hoogstraaten was clearly delighted by this oddity of the human eye, not the least troubled by the fact that he could not explain it.

Walking behind Father and Mijnheer van Hoogstraaten, I tilted my head this way and that, so that I saw the world sideways, and I wondered how my eyes knew what to do about it. Was the boy up inside my head, his hoop down? Or the other way around? And where was the sky?

I did not ask, for Mijnheer van Hoogstraaten was already speaking of other things. He did not stop until we reached the house where the room was and Father said, "We are here." He grew very quiet then. We all went up the stairs together, and Father paused at the closed door. "Will you see the painting first, Samuel, or shall I go in and close the shutters so that you can first see the image cast on the wall?"

"Oh, the painting to be sure," said Mijnheer van Hoogstraaten without a moment's hesitation. "It is the painting I've come all the way from Dordrecht to see."

"Well, then."

Father opened the door and Mijnheer van Hoogstraaten breathed in sharply when he stepped inside. Still holding his big leather bag, he walked to the painting and stood before it. He looked a long time, raised his free hand now and then as if to capture in it what he saw. "Oh," he said. "Oh, my."

Then he set the bag on the floor and looked at Father, his eyes shining. "What you have done, Jan—it *is* a wonder. This rose tint to the sand! The way the light gathers on the boat! And, oh, this yellow roof!" He looked out the window at the real view, then at the painting again. "How did you know to make it just so? Close the shutters now, and let me see what the lens shows you."

I closed my eyes and listened to Father's footsteps cross the room. I heard the shutters close. The dark behind my eyelids grew darker. I raised my hand like a blind person, floated it away from me until my fingertips could sense the canvas beneath them; then I opened my eyes and looked to see what part of the town the light had painted on my outstretched hand. This was a game I liked to play when Father closed the shutters to study the view, and today I saw on my hand one of the herring boats docked on the quay. I made other things appear on it, too, just moving it along the wall: trees, water, people. The twin turrets of the Rotterdam Gate.

When I stood on tiptoe to reach for the bell tower of the Nieuwe Kerk, the bells inside the real tower suddenly rang out from across the town. I pulled my hand back then, and put it in my pocket. I felt foolish at the way my heart was racing, glad that Father and Mijnheer van Hoogstraaten had forgotten about me. They were no more than voices speaking in the dark.

"Truly, Jan, this is magnificent. So large and real. Ah, the way the light moves on the water! And what beautiful distortions! Will van Leeuwenhoek join us at Mechelen so he can explain how he went about crafting the lens to make them so?"

"If we fetch him there," Father said. "He will not remember, left to his own devices. Poor man! He deserves a good meal for all his efforts. First there was nothing but a blur of color: too large. Then the image was too small and sharp. So he is grinding, looking, grinding until—what you see."

"And all the while complaining," Mijnheer Hoogstraaten said.

"Yes, complaining." Father laughed. "If he were not complaining, how would we know him?" He opened the shutters, flooded the room with light, and Mijnheer van Hoogstraaten went to the painting again.

"Van Ruijven, has he seen it?"

"No. He will wait until it is finished."

"And then it will go directly to his house?"

"Yes," Father said.

Mijnheer van Hoogstraaten shook his head, bemused. "A shame," he said. "I should like to see it in Amsterdam, or The Hague. I should like to hear what people would say about it."

Father was quiet.

"You do not care, do you, Jan? How is it that your friends care more than you do that your work should be known?"

"Van Ruijven pays me well for my work," Father said. "That is what I care about. To paint what I want to paint and to be paid well for it, what more can a man ask?"

It was exactly the same thing he said to Grandmother Thins when she complained about how slowly he worked, how impractical he was about the business of painting. She was always trying to convince him to make *more* pictures. Her friend, Mijnheer de Coge—a good Catholic—would take them to Amsterdam, she said, where someone other than Mijnheer van Ruijven could buy them. What use were a few paintings hung on the wall of one man's home? Who would ever see them? How would Father's reputation grow if he had but one patron?

If Mijnheer van Hoogstraaten also felt this way, he did not say so. He just thumped Father on the back and said again that his *View of Delft* was a wondrous, wondrous thing. A marvel! And I felt myself puff up, as if I had had some part in making it myself. As if I had pulled the light beams through Mijnheer van Leeuwenhoek's lens and spread them on the canvas with my own fingers.

✛ ✛ ✛ ✛ ✛

I ran ahead to Mechelen, surprising Grandma Digna in the kitchen, throwing my arms around her waist. "Father told Grandmother Thins that I must come and help you with the meal," I said. "And Cornelia kindly agreed to take on my duties so that I might do so. Are you not happy to see me?"

"Ah, little one," she said, tipping my face up with her finger.

I laughed and scolded her gently. "I am not so little anymore, Grandma. Father lets me work for him now. Look." I spread my hands to show her the crescent moons of madder lake pigment beneath my fingernails. "I have been grinding all morning!"

"Well." She spread out her own floury hands. "I have been working all morning, too, making your *hutsepot*. And your apple custard. So we are alike, yes?"

She glanced up then, saw Father striding through the doorway, his arms open to receive her, and her expression brought to my mind a painting from Italy that hung in the home of our Jesuit brothers: pink and white angels looking upwards, their faces filled with joy.

I left them to help Jutte, Grandma's kitchen maid, carry out the meal. There was a big plate of herring, with chopped onions. *Broodjes* and cheese. The *hutsepot* straight from the cooking fire.

A number of Father's fellow painters from the St. Luke's Guild and Mijnheer van Hoogstraaten were already seated at the round wooden table in the corner of the tavern. Mijnheer van Leeuwenhoek had folded himself into his chair, and he was waving his long arms excitedly, telling Mijnheer van Hoogstraaten what he had most recently seen in his lenses.

"A mosquito wing! The eye of a bee, the leg of a louse." He plucked a hair from his head and laid it on the palm of his hand. "Look here," he said. "This one hair is twenty-five times the size of the flea's sting. One hair! What do you think of that?"

But before Mijnheer van Hoogstraaten could answer, he went on, bemoaning how little time he was given to do his work. There was his drapery shop to be attended to, every day but Sunday. Endless, mindless measuring and cutting of cloth. And his duties at Town Hall, where he examined weights and measures. He must work late into the night, straining his eyes terribly in the candlelight, if he were to continue looking at bits and pieces of the world through his microscopes.

Mijnheer van Hoogstraaten winked at me. "Ah, yes, it is a terrible life." He picked up a silver herring by its tail, dipped it in the chopped onion and devoured it in one bite. "Would that we were able to spend every minute with our paints or lenses, leaving only to come here to Mechelen, where we are served Digna's good food by the beautiful Jutte whenever we grow hungry!" Old Mijnheer Bramer smiled and raised his glass to her.

Blushing, Jutte filled it and the others with wine from her pewter pitcher. When Father came in from the kitchen, we ate—both Grandma Digna and Jutte hovering near the table, attending to our every need. Even Mijnheer van Leeuwenhoek grew quiet, consuming a huge bowl of *hutespot* with the battered spoon he had carried with him in his pocket. I loved Grandma Digna's *hutespot* more than any food in the world. The bits of beef and onion so tender, the flavor of ginger bursting on my tongue. Whenever I ate it, I remembered the story Father told of the siege of Leiden. Months and months, the cruel Spanish soldiers had held the town, until finally the town regents decided to open the dykes and flood it rather than to have it remain in foreign hands. The sea surged through fields where the Spanish army had set up its camps, and frightened the soldiers away. When the waters receded, a small boy crept into their deserted garrison and found one fire still miraculously burning—an iron cauldron of *hutespot* left cooking on it.

We should be proud to be Dutch, Father always said, telling the story. We were strong, good people who loved our land and everything in it. In the evenings, he taught us children about our country and the whole world from the big maps he kept rolled up in his painting room. I liked best the one of our own town, for when I looked at the lines and shapes on it, what I knew they stood for sprang up in my mind's eye. Canals, streets, marketplaces, harbors. Great Markt Square with Mechelen on one side and Grandmother Thins's house on the other, in the far corner.

I meant to see the places on all of Father's other maps someday. Every town in Holland, and even far-off Africa. I would sneak aboard a ship, perhaps, and go there. And to the Orient, as well, where I would make a great collection of oddities, and drink green tea for the first time. Indeed, I should drink it to my heart's content!

But for now I was content to be at Mechelen, Grandma Digna's friendly dogs begging table scraps, her parrot squawking in its cage, as if to add its own thoughts to the spirited talk between Father and his friends. When the *hutsepot* and herring were gone, when there was nothing left of Grandma's apple custard, the men prepared their pipes for a long drink of tobacco and soon smoke swirled above the table like silver fog.

Finally we were to see what Mijnheer van Hoogstraaten had brought. He lifted his leather bag to the table, opened it, and took out a wooden box. It is just a *camera obscura*, I thought with disappointment. The kind Mijnheer van Leeuwenhoek had made for Father to examine the effects of light in his painting room.

"Carelina," said Mijnheer van Hoogstraaten. "You shall have the first look."

I expected to look into the top and see whatever image of the tavern the light had carried to the glass inside. But Mijnheer van Hoogstraaten directed me to a peep-hole on the side of the box, and when I looked through it I was surprised to find before me what looked like the inside of a *poppenhuis*. There were rooms leading into rooms, chairs as real as the chair I had been sitting on, a sleeping cupboard heaped with blankets, a black-framed mirror tilting away from the wall. There was a woman sitting in the corner, near a window, reading a letter.

Mijnheer van Hoogstraaten leaned down so that his face was next to mine. "Look closely, *dochterken*," he said. "Look for the mirrors."

And I saw them! I saw, too, how cleverly he had placed them so that the black and white tile floor was reflected, enlarged, and the chairs and sleeping cupboard that he had painted flat on the wall seemed to jut out from it. An open door was painted on one side of the box and mirrored on the side opposite, tricking the viewer's eye into believing there was a whole room beyond. I blinked and the scene before me once again looked perfectly natural: three separate rooms in a *poppenhuis*, opening one into the next. It made my head ache to consider how both the mirrors and the illusion they made could seem equally real.

I called Grandma Digna to look, then Jutte. Both stepped back, their hands to their hearts. Then the men looked. First Father, who was delighted by it. Then quiet Mijnheer de Witte, who looked a long time, then sat down and closed his eyes, as if to paint it all over again inside his head. Mijnheer van Leeuwenhoek had a thousand questions, which Mijnheer van Hoogstraaten answered by handing him a sheaf of papers from the bag. They were full of angles and numbers, which Mijnheer van Leeuwenhoek peered at through his spectacles, muttering to himself. With grudging admiration, he handed them back.

He was a scientist, after all. His work was to look closely the world and describe it so that the eye might know what it saw. He found it hard to approve of fooling the eye, which was the painter's task. It seemed a terrible waste of time to him, when there was so much around us yet to be understood. But, as always, Mijnheer van Hoog-straaten took pleasure in reminding him that the painter understands the nature of things every bit as well as a scientist, for he must understand by what means the eye is fooled. I looked into the peep-box while they argued, Father and his fellow painters chiming in, and I pretended that I was living in that miniature world while the real world swirled around me in words.

✛✛✛✛✛✛✛✛✛✛✛✛✛✛✛✛✛✛✛✛✛✛✛✛✛✛✛✛✛

# WOMAN HOLDING A BALANCE

✛✛✛✛✛✛✛✛✛✛✛✛✛✛✛✛✛✛✛✛✛✛✛✛✛✛✛✛✛

UR MOTHER had been feeling weak and listless for several weeks; and Tanneke bid her breathe in the fumes of a smoldering cord, for if it made her ill it would be a sure sign that she was with child again. Despite Grandmother's annoyance at such an old-fashioned superstition, it was soon enough proven true, and as the baby grew within her Mother became fretful at the prospect of another long lying-in. Nothing could please her. Not Maria playing her best-loved compositions on the virginal; not the pretty bouquets of flowers that Cornelia picked for her out in the fields; not the young capons or the flaky fish drenched in butter that Tanneke made to tempt and nourish her. She ate these things only because Grandmother pressed them upon her, reminding her that the womb of a woman her age had likely begun to dry up. It needed softening with the oils that such rich foods provided if it were to properly nourish the baby inside.

This invariably made Mother cry. She sat at her dressing table, staring at herself in the mirror, as if she could not believe what she saw there. The rich food had already begun to put weight on her, even padding the bones of her face. Her stomach swelled so that her clothes no longer fit her. She felt nauseated and light-headed much of the time, and so spent hour upon hour lying miserably abed.

Grandmother seemed half-angry attending her, as if it were

laziness that kept her there. In fact, it seemed to me that Grand-mother was angry that Mother was with child at all. Surely, though, this could not be possible, for children came at the will of God, and His will must not be questioned.

Then, there were so many things I did not understand. Why, for instance, had God blessed Father with so many children, when he had sent his sister, our Aunt Gertruy, but one and then called him back to heaven before he was weaned? Why, since this blessing of children that He had given us required Grandmother Thins's assist-ance, had He not rewarded her generosity by granting her a calm and happy spirit, so that she might enjoy us instead of being cross and anxious in our presence?

Thankfully, Mother brightened and took strength as autumn neared; and by the first day of the kermis, she felt well enough to accompany us children to the fair. A half-hour past midday, the bells on the clock tower began to peal. All morning, we had watched the tradespeople hurry past our house on their way to Great Markt Square, where they would set up tents and stalls to display their wares. Pottery, cloth, glass and silver trinkets, souvenirs. And wonderful food. My mouth watered to think of the waffles and pancakes, the sausages and ham pies. Kermis cakes with pink sugar icing.

The bells were still ringing wildly when we ventured out into the streets to watch Father in the parade: Mother, Maria, Elisabeth, Cornelia, Beatrix, Aleydis, and I. Like nearly every housemaid in Delft, Tanneke had left for the festival after preparing the morning meal. Grandmother had kindly agreed to look after the baby, Gretje. She never went to kermis for fear of encountering our Uncle Willem there.

Mother feared him, too. But Father had convinced her to walk across the square and join him at Mechelen, where, he assured her, she would be safe. She was beautiful in the blue dress Tanneke had altered to allow for the child growing within her, and she seemed calm for the first time in a long while. Her heart light. She directed our attention to the world around us. The sky, blue as a Delft plate. The scent of dying roses. Still green, the drying, heart-shaped leaves of the linden trees rustled above us. One and then another danced down, swirling in the light breeze: gentle reminders that winter was on the way. But the warmth of the September sun allowed us to deny it.

In the distance, the flutes and drums of the militia could be heard. The members had begun their march through the streets of the town, and soon appeared, the drummers at the head of the column, the officers behind them, their helmets shining in the sun. And then the artisans, dressed in the colorful costumes of their guilds. As one of the headmen of the St. Luke's Guild, Father led his fellow guildsmen, bearing their flag. We called to him and he smiled in our direction.

Once in the square, the militia gathered at the open place in the center, where a post had been set up, topped with a painted wooden parrot. The soldiers drew lots, then one by one, each drew his bow and took a turn at trying to knock the bird down with his arrow. With much laughter and cheering, the first to accomplish this was proclaimed master marksman of the kermis, crowned with a fancy hat of feathers, and then strolled along the square, taking his time to choose one of the prettiest girls to be his companion for the duration of the fair. He strutted and smiled, drank from the glass of ale someone had thrust into his hand.

Maria watched, her face flushed with excitement, no doubt dreaming that she might be chosen for such an honor some day. She must have known Grandmother would never allow this. Still, I had seen her primp before the mirror that very morning, pinch her cheeks and lips to redden them. I imagined her a few years from now, her body grown womanly as Tanneke promised it would, and I wondered if then she would find herself out of grace with our grandmother. She had never been so yet, and took every opportunity to chastise me when my actions caused Grandmother distress.

But I would not think of that now. Aleydis was tugging at my hand. Cornelia and I had promised to take her and Beatrix to the toy stall so that they might spend the coins that Father had given them this morning. I glanced at Mother, who gave her consent, bidding us to be careful and to hurry straight to Mechelen when we were through.

But I walked slowly with my sisters, drinking in the fair. Kermis singers roamed the streets; fiddlers fiddled; agents sang out rhymed praises of their masters' wares. At the toy stall, there were dolls and penny whistles. Whirligigs, hoops, hobby horses, soldiers carved of wood. Aleydis chose a doll; Beatrix, a little tin horn, which she tooted determinedly as we made our winding way to Mechelen, stopping to look at whatever pleased us.

There were tight-ope walkers and acrobats, talking dogs and sum-adding horses, healers and fortune tellers. We three drew close to one another at the sight of the rat catcher, holding forth a collection of the most recent victims of his arsenic cakes hung by their tails on a line. And again, watching the bee-keeper show how his thousands of buzzing bees returned to their hive at his command.

At the bakers' stalls, young men gathered to buy kermis cakes for girls they admired. The flat oval cakes had messages written on them: *For Your Kermis. With My Love.* I hoped Tanneke might receive one, for I knew it would please her. But selfishly I hoped she would eat the whole cake herself. Then when her suitor came to see her on the second Sunday after kermis and found that she had not saved a slice for him, he would know she did not wish to marry him. Tanneke was so dear to me. I wanted her to stay with us forever.

At Mechelen, there were long tables set outside and barrels for the patrons to sit on, drinking their tankards of beer. Father and

Mother sat on the end of one of the tables, his arm around her shoulders. Maria and Elisabeth sat beside them, eating *poffertjes*. Grandma Digna gave me a quick hug, then Aleydis, Beatrix, and Cornelia. "Sit, lambkins," she said, and bade Jutte to bring us some of the little pancakes, too. We ate them—as many as we wanted—our fingers sticky with the sugar icing, melting lumps of butter running down our arms.

As the afternoon passed, Father's friends from the St. Luke's Guild gathered at our table, gesturing widely, painting pictures with their words. All around us, people danced on the cobblestones. Dogs barked. Children chased each other, ducking among the tables, laughing and shouting. Cats skulked and begged for scraps.

Revelers kept pouring into Great Markt Square from the nearby passageway across the Voldersgracht. Girls a few years older than Maria, in pretty dresses and starched caps, arms linked, heads bent, whispering secrets. Crowds of unruly boys, pummeling and jostling one another, looking to make mischief. One boy held a live goose aloft, another carried a coiled rope over his shoulder. When they found the right spot, they might stretch the rope from tree to tree across the street and hang the goose from its feet in the center. They'd take turns racing at full speed to where the goose hung, jump up and try to grab its greased neck. Or they might hang the goose by its feet from a tree limb, then blindfolded, armed with knives, take turns trying to sever its neck.

Our Uncle Willem, Mother's brother, had played such cruel games at the kermis in Gouda when he was a boy. I had heard Grandmother speak of it to Mother once, after having an unpleasant encounter with him in the street. He had been indulged in every kind of bad behavior by his father, she said, who from the day of Willem's birth had refused to reprimand him for anything. He was a violent man himself. Once, when Grandmother punished Uncle Willem for some offense, our grandfather was so angry that he pulled his own daughter—our mother—through the house by the hair and beat her soundly. "I shall do it every time you beat my son!" he shouted at Grandmother when he was through.

He had often beaten Grandmother as well. He had taken all of the money that had come to her through her family and hidden it, so that she must beg him for every penny she needed—even to buy food for the family and sand to scour the pots and clean the floors with. Often he became so violent toward her that she must seek haven at her sister's house. She left him finally, after the time he hit and kicked her viciously and chased her out the door and down the street with a fire tong. Witless with fear for her own life, she had abandoned poor Mother that morning. Grandfather put her in the care of a neighbor, then later locked her in the garden house, where Grandmother and our Aunt Cornelia had found her hours later crying piteously.

It was then that Grandmother and Mother moved to Delft. Our grandfather and Willem stayed in Gouda, and Willem was forbidden to visit his mother. He traveled to Delft from time to time, nonetheless—though only to torment Grandmother and demand money which he believed rightly belonged to him. Mother, his sister, was frightened of him, for he was much like her father, who had treated her so badly when she was a girl. He would likely come to Delft some time during kermis; he usually did. If we spotted him, Father told us children, we must turn away before he caught sight of us and return home at once. But here at Grandma Digna's, all together under the warm September sun, we need not fear him. Indeed, we stayed so long and late that Father must carry Aleydis home on his strong shoulders.

The next day Mother felt poorly again, and Grandmother sent us children outside so we would not disturb her. We were told not to venture past the Molenpoort, not to go anywhere near the square where the kermis revelers had grown more bawdy. We were to stay away from the canal as well. Since the beginning of kermis yesterday, two people were already known drowned, one of them a boy of six, who had been knocked into the water when he got in the way of a scuffle.

Maria and Elisabeth sat in a shady corner, talking in whispers. Cornelia spun Aleydis's top and gathered pebbles for her to mix with dirt and serve on little dishes to her dolls. But I felt languid and melancholy, and could bring myself to do no more than watch people pass by on their way to the fair.

My first sight of the absurd man swaggering and lurching along Oude Langendyjk made me smile. His yellow hair was wild, his long white shirt tail flapped behind him like a flag, and he waved a big stick, as if there were cattle and not people surging around him. Then I saw that it was our Uncle Willem. I stood instantly to go warn Grandmother, but it was too late. In a long, quick bound, he was before me, grinning.

"Ah, Carelina," he said. Then, including my sisters with a sweep of his hand, "I see that my dear mother has exiled the whole lot of you urchins to the street. Where is she, the good Vrouw Thins? I have come to pay her a visit."

"Inside, Uncle," I said. I knew the door was not locked, and I moved to place myself in front of it. "I shall go get her for you."

But he stepped around me, knocking me off-balance, and pound-ed his fist on the door. Then, before Grandmother could come, he entered, shouting for her.

I followed him, watched him stride through the front hall, into the front room. Mother was resting there, I knew, hidden behind the drawn curtains of her sleeping cupboard. Grandmother was there, too, at the open linen cupboard, putting away the freshly pressed bedclothes. She went about her business calmly, as if she were completely unaware of Uncle Willem in the doorway, his stick raised. She closed the cupboard, locked it with one of the keys from the ring of household keys she kept with her always.

Uncle Willem muttered, "She-devil!"

Grandmother turned to him. "Have you been drinking, Willem?" she asked.

"It is kermis," Uncle Willem said.

Grandmother raised an eyebrow. "I am aware of that."

He gave her an impish grin. "Then it should not surprise you to know that I am in need of funds. I have come to beg your indulgence."

"I cannot indulge your desire to become more debauched than you appear now, before me, Willem."

Uncle Willem laughed. "You *will not* indulge me," he said. "I am your son, after all—but do you feel even the smallest desire to please me?" He mimicked her voice. "*I cannot indulge you.* Well then, I shall indulge myself; and to do so I ask of you only what is mine."

Grandmother fingered the leather purse, which hung from her waist. He took a step toward her, his palm turned up to receive the coins. But his attention was deflected when she glanced anxiously at Mother's sleeping cupboard. Quick as a hare, he swept past her, struck at the green silk curtains with his stick.

"Nor does my own sister have any concern for my happiness," he said bitterly when she did not emerge. "Indeed, she will not even acknowledge my presence. Catharina!" He struck the curtains again, then pulled them open, and I saw Mother huddled in the far corner, trembling, her hands covering her face.

"Catharina," he repeated.

She would not look at him.

He poked at her swollen stomach with his stick. "So this is where all our Mother's money is to be spent then. More babies. You and your poor painter do not seem to know how to stop having them."

"Willem," Grandmother said.

"Ah," he laughed. "Now you will give it to me. Now that I threaten your precious Catharina."

White-faced, Grandmother took a gold coin from her purse.

Uncle Willem pocketed it, his eyes glittering with malice. "You think you are finished with me now? You think now you have given me what is owed me I will simply go? Well, I shall go," he said. "But not alone. I wish to take my dear sister with me. Come, Catharina. Make haste! We shall go to the kermis together and drink until we become friends at last."

He grabbed Mother's arm and forced her, weeping, from the bed.

"No, Willem," she said. "Please. I must stay here with the children. Listen. Gretje is crying in the next room. You have awakened her. And poor Carelina, look, you have frightened her to death."

He tightened his grip on her arm, causing her to gasp. "Then we shall take Gretje and Carelina with us," he said. "And I shall make them laugh. We shall all be friends." He turned to me. "Do you not wish to be my friend, Carelina? Have I not always been kind to you?"

I opened my mouth, but no sound came out. I wanted nothing more than to bolt and run from the house, out into the street where the others had had the good sense to stay. But my feet would not work any better than my tongue.

Uncle Willem moved toward me, Mother stumbling, still in his grasp. Grandmother stood, still as a statue, her hand on her heart. Then Tanneke appeared in the doorway. She had been to the market and still had her basket, full of vegetables, over her arm. Without a moment's hesitation, she swung it hard. Carrots and cabbages flew in every direction. Uncle Willem's stick clattered to the floor. When he bent to pick it up, she set upon him with a fierceness I had never seen in her, raining blow after blow upon his head and shoulders until he must let go of Mother to protect himself.

Still, Tanneke continued to batter him, and though he called her all manner of blasphemous names, trying to frighten her off, she did not stop until she had backed him out of the room, into the front hallway, and out the door, where my sisters were crying and a crowd of neighbors and passersby had gathered, having heard the ruckus inside. Grandmother threw his stick after him. It clattered on the cobblestones. With all the dignity he could muster, Uncle Willem picked it up and wove down Oude Langendyjk on his way to the fair.

Inside, Mother was still trembling. We children gathered round her, and she drew us near, murmuring our names, giving us little kisses light as breath. Pressed against her belly, I imagined the new baby rippling like a fish inside her. Had it heard Uncle Willem shouting, I wondered? Had it felt our Mother's fear? Could it feel *me* nestling ever closer, hoping to bring comfort?

Tanneke made Spinach with Soldiers to calm us children: strips of fried bread standing upright in a warm, buttery field of spinach. It was our favorite dish, but Uncle Willem had frightened us so badly that we could not enjoy it. Only the baby, Gretje, ate heartily, apparently having already forgotten his loud, threatening voice.

I knew I should never forget it myself—nor the sight of Mother when he drew back the curtains of her sleeping cupboard. Grandmother must have felt the same way. She bade a neighbor cross the square and fetch Father from Mechelen, but did not even wait for his arrival before retiring to her own quarters upstairs. There she rested, a glass of wine at her bedside, a cool cloth soaked in rosewater upon her brow.

When Father finally appeared, Mother burst into tears, and

Tanneke had to explain what had happened. His face, already grim, darkened; and, I think, if Mother had not needed him so, he would have gone in search of Uncle Willem. But toward what end? I could not imagine our gentle father harming anyone. Indeed, his anger dissolved quickly into an expression of sadness and concern. He held Mother close to him until her tears ceased. Then he took her hand and led her upstairs to his painting room, where they often went if they wanted to talk quietly, alone.

But they were not talking when, some time later, I crept up the stairs and peered into the room. Mother stood before him, perfectly still, a white cowl upon her head, its white tips resting on her shoulders. She stood perfectly still, holding a set of brass scales lightly between her thumb and finger.

He was going to paint her again. I knew this by the way he looked at her, now and then reaching out to touch her. He tilted her head so that the cowl fell prettily around her face; he lowered one of her shoulders slightly, placed the fingers of her empty hand on the edge of the table. He bade her put on her yellow morning jacket with the ermine trim, then arranged it to fall open over the curve of her belly, revealing the bright orange ribbons trailing from her bodice.

I was glad that Grandmother had taken to her bed and closed her door, for I knew she did not like to see Father arranging our mother this way. It was shameful in her view, though I did not understand why. How could she fail to see the love in Father's eyes those times he discovered in Mother something that he wanted to paint? How could she fail to see the way Mother was calmed and strengthened by his touch? As for myself, I watched from my shadowy place in the hallway, bereft, for I knew it meant Father and I would not return to the room above the harbor until he had finished this new painting of our mother.

In the next days, the painting grew beneath Father's brush. He worked quickly, wet on wet, and our mother's face emerged from shadow to substance as she might have emerged, standing there before the window as night changed to day.

Then Father bade me grind and prepare red ochre, which he painted in a thin layer where I knew Mother's yellow jacket would be. This seemed odd until, next, I ground and prepared the ultramarine with charcoal for him and saw, with his first brushstrokes, that he meant to make the jacket blue, an even darker blue than the blue cloth that lay in shadow on the table. I marveled at his choices, and it seemed to me that God might have made each one of us in this manner, applying His great brush to the canvas of earth.

I marveled, too, at his obliviousness to Grandmother Thins's anger. She went about the house, muttering about the foolishness of postponing the completion of a commissioned work. It was shameful to make such an excellent patron as Mijnheer van Ruijven wait for what he desired, she said.

But there was no arguing with Father when a vision compelled him. It was as if he had no choice in the matter; he must paint what his mind's eye saw. And he was never happier than when he was in the midst of such a work.

Again and again, he took Mother from her household chores so that he could look at her. I watched him drape the rich blue cloth on the left foreground of the table. On the bare wood, he set the large jewelry box and several small ones, a gold chain, several strands of pearls. These things he incessantly arranged and rearranged—-moving back and forth to his small *camera obscura* to consider the effect

Grandmother's ill will and grumbling only made him behave

more kindly to her than usual, to be more diligent in helping her attend to her affairs during the hours when he was not working at his easel. He teased Tanneke. He was endlessly patient with the little ones, whittling flutes from scraps of wood and teaching them to play songs on them. He made Mother blush with his ardent affection.

If he noticed the subtle ways in which Grandmother turned her displeasure upon me, he did not acknowledge it. She bade me care for the little ones without Cornelia's help, and serve my sister Maria as if I were her maidservant. Afternoons, when I was finished in the painting room, I was not allowed to run errands for Tanneke, but must stay indoors, knitting, until my fingers ached. Anger simmered inside me, but I kept it in check for I knew that Grandmother was watching, waiting for a show of temper so that she might go to Father with a complaint.

Nights, I dreamed myself flying—Father's *View of Delft* beneath me, blue and gold and shining. By some magic, I swooped down and flew into it, entering through the Scheidam Gate. I skimmed along the canals, never touching the surface of the water; then rose to view the reflections the arched bridges made, and they seemed to me as lovely, as elusive as a strand of painted pearls. Brimming with happiness, I soared upward to where the canals were no more than silver threads and Grandmother's house was not even visible.

So vivid was this recurring dream that I felt quite untethered to the real Delft into which I awoke each morning. Climbing the stairs to the painting room, I must brace myself with the palm of my hand; entering, I must stand in the doorway and look round the room, as if to remember it. There was the table, draped with blue cloth, the wood jewelry boxes, the pearls. The grinding slab, the stone. Light streaming through the mullioned windows. Father at his easel, deeply absorbed in his work.

The painting was nearly finished: Mother fully alive on the

canvas, contemplating the balance she held lightly in her right hand. Behind her, taking up half of the gray wall, Father had painted *The Last Judgment* in black and ochre, the bottom of it writhing with doomed souls. Our Lord was at the top, haloed, near Mother's head—as if she were thinking of Him. As if He were the cause of her serenity amidst such darkness. The only light in the painting seeped in through the top of a gold curtain, brightening a section of the gray wall, the suspended pans of the scale Mother held, and the orange ribbon of her bodice. It illuminated the white fur trim on her jacket and her white cap, caused the gilded edges of the *The Last Judgment*'s ebony frame to shine.

Entering one morning, still half-dreaming, I raised my hand toward it. Father turned at the sound of my footstep, and I saw in his smile that he knew what I was thinking.

"See how the white frames her face," he said.

I saw this. And how invisible lines from her eyes led to the vanishing point, then on down to the pearls and the gold chain on the table. But where was the light coming from that made these things shine? It seemed to me that they should have fallen in shadow.

I made this observation to Father with hesitation, for fear of seeming stupid. Or worse, offending him. So I was much relieved see on his face the pleasure my words brought.

"Ah, Carelina," he said. "It is true. There is no source for the light you see, no source at all. The pearls, the gold should not shine. And therein lies the heart of things. The difference between what is here, in the real world, before us—and what we see."

✢ ✢ ✢ ✢ ✢

Sometimes I wondered if Father might rather live in the peaceful world he made in his paintings than in the real world of Delft, with all its noise and commotion and so many people desirous of his time. Now that the painting of our mother was finished and, thankfully, purchased by Mijnheer van Ruiven for his collection, he must attend to the duties he had set aside while he was consumed by his vision. He must travel to Gouda to skirmish with Uncle Willem over one of Grandmother Thins's properties there. He must help Grandma Digna with her Mechelen accounts, and tend to his own business of buying and selling fine arts objects, which augmented the limited income he was able to generate practicing his craft. He must fulfill his obligations as one of the headmen at the St. Luke Guild.

It was deep autumn when he finally returned to his *View of Delft*. The air was cold; the trees looked like big paint brushes tipped with paint—red, yellow, orange. It was still summer in the painting, though. The leaves on the trees were green. The sky was blue and white, with only one dark cloud. The sun was shining.

I had so looked forward to our return to the painting room above the harbor, longed for the quiet mornings I had shared with my father there; but gregarious Mijnheer van Hoogstraaten had trumpeted the marvels of the painting in his endless travels about the republic, and we were often interrupted by visitors. Father's friend, Mijnheer de Hoogh, traveled from Amsterdam to see it; Mijnheers Dou and van Mieris came from Leiden.

Then he received word that Lord Constantin Huygens meant to travel from The Hague to our town so that he might see this work that had lately become the main topic of conversation of those in our capitol who admired the art of painting.

Father was honored, of course, and hoped the visit might result in a commission. Grandmother was determined that it should be so, for a painting displayed in the home of Lord Huygens would be seen and admired by the richest, most influential men of our time.

On the morning he and his party were to visit the painting room, she hovered over Tanneke in the kitchen, directing her preparation of the refreshments one way and then another until finally Tanneke threw up her hands and burst into tears. That only made Grandmother redouble her efforts toward perfection. The herring must presented just so on the silver platter. The wine must be kept cool in the cellar until the last possible moment. And Tanneke must stop crying at once! She must not appear puffy and red-faced when serving the refreshments. Grandmother soaked a cloth in cold water and bade her press it against her eyes.

She fretted over me as well. At Father's insistence, I would be present for the regent's visit; and once Grandmother was resigned to this, she determined that I must make a decent appearance. One of Maria's dresses had been cut down to fit me, and now she slipped it over my head and fussed it into place. She brushed my hair until my scalp felt as if it were on fire, then tied on my cap, which had been starched so stiffly that its sharp edges bit into my skin. She bade me practice my curtsy until my legs ached from the strain.

Cornelia stood by me in this, a comforting presence. Maria watched from the doorway. She disdained the tasks I did joyfully for our father, ridiculed my paint-stained hands. It was boys' work, she said. Unsuitable. But it was for this work that Father had chosen me to accompany him for Lord Huygens's visit, and I could sense the envy behind her careful, bored expression. I sensed it, too, in Elisabeth's pious concern.

"I shall pray for you, Carelina," she said. "That you may be capable of acting rightly in the presence of such a great man."

I thanked her sweetly, as if kindness had prompted her remark; but I must confess an exquisite pleasure in the knowledge that it had not. Indeed, my sense of anticipation was greater for my sisters' envy; and I set out with Father in high spirits. Tanneke followed with the refreshments on a borrowed pull-cart; and as our little procession made its way through *Papenhoek*, our neighbors called out, bidding us good fortune.

The painting room above the harbor gleamed, for Tanneke had been the day before to give it a good cleaning. When we had carried the refreshments upstairs and she had arranged them on the table to Father's satisfaction, he dismissed her with thanks.

"Carelina shall serve," he said.

Tanneke heaved a sigh of relief. She had been sleepless with dread for nights, and was grateful to be excused from such great responsibility. But I felt myself flush at the thought of what Grandmother would say when Tanneke returned and told her that Father had allowed me the privilege of serving such honored guests. After all, hadn't I proven myself completely incapable of the gentle arts that Mejuffrouw van Aeckel had pained to teach me? Perhaps Tanneke sensed my apprehension, for she drew me to her in a quick hug before leaving.

"You shall do a fine job, Carelina," she declared. "Were he not certain of it, your father would not give you the task."

"Yes. This is so," he said.

I drew myself up then, determined to be worthy of his trust in me.

The regent and his party arrived at the house on the harbor promptly at the appointed hour, and shook Father's hand. They had met on several occasions at The Hague, when Father had gone there to do business for the guild; and I felt proud to see Father at ease with someone so grand. Prouder still to be acknowledged as his helper.

"My daughter, Carelina," Father said, his hand on my shoulder. "She is named for Fabritius, my mentor and friend, and she is lately of great assistance to me when I paint."

Lord Huygens turned his intense gaze upon me. He was a small, neat man. His gray beard was groomed to a sharp point; his moustache was twisted up at the ends; his features were angular. A pair of silver spectacles was perched on his nose. Here was a man privy to the lives of kings and princes, I thought. Poor and plain as I was, I should have been disconcerted by his attention. But I was not. If Father believed me worthy of it, then I must be. I held my head high, made a perfect curtsy before him.

He smiled and nodded, then introduced both Father and me to the men who accompanied him: an ambassador, a regent, and a member of Parliament. All dressed in black, their coattails flapping, they were like a flock of crows ascending the stairs to the painting room.

Once inside the room, Lord Huygens went directly to the painting and stood before it. An odd sound came up from his throat, not unlike the cooing sound little Gretje made, nursing at our mother's breast. When he had looked a long time, he turned to Father. "I have seen and admired other work you have done for Mijnheer van Ruijven," he said. "This surpasses it."

Father gave a little nod. "You are kind."

Lord Huygens smiled. "I have never learned how to be kind about a work of art, Mijnheer Vermeer. My heart betrays me. Here—" He gestured to his three friends to draw closer and, having looked at the painting just once, delivered a brief but astute lecture on its composition and perspective, in which he proved what he had just said was true.

After Father demonstrated the workings of Mijnheer van Leeuwenhoek's lens and answered our guests' questions about it, I served the refreshments. When the wine was poured, Lord Huygens proposed a toast to Father's good work, and the men raised their glasses. Then he spoke to Father about a painting he wished to commission. It was to be a gift for his son, Christiaan, a renowned scientist and mathematician, to celebrate his fortieth year. Lord Huygens was deeply proud of his son's accomplishments, and wanted the painting that he hoped Father would paint to be a reflection of the young man's intellectual gifts. The actual subject and composition would be left to Father's imagination. And, of course, he understood that Father must complete Mijnheer van Ruijven's painting before beginning the new work.

Father quickly agreed to his generous terms. I poured more wine, served the herring, then found a quiet place near the window where I could sit, unnoticed, and listen. Their talk was spirited. Lord Huygens spoke passionately about his belief that the new science allowed man to more fully explore and discover God's great plan. We must not fear knowledge. Would God have given us the means to learn had he not wished for us to do so?

"It is true that the classics have much to teach us," he said. "We would be fools to disregard them. "But—" He tapped the silver rim of his spectacles. "Lenses are something the Greeks did not understand. And without these spectacles, I should see no more than the most ignorant man!"

The men murmured in agreement. For Lord Huygen's great intelligence, the fruits of his devoted service to our republic to have been lost for want of the new science surely proved its worth! I doubted Grandmother would agree. Awed as she had been by news of the regent's visit, I knew that she believed the new science to be a kind of sorcery. She crossed herself when Father forgot himself and, excited about some new idea, spoke of it at her table.

It made me a little sad to see Father among these men. To see the eagerness with which he entered the discussion that ranged from the increasingly dire relations with England to Marisius's new book about the abuses of Cartesian philosophy. If there had not been so many of us, if Mother had been stronger, if it had not been necessary to for us live with our Grandmother to make ends meet, he might have left Delft and established himself in The Hague or Amsterdam, where his work and his intelligence would be appreciated, where he would be able to engage in such conversation every day. There were only a few really good painters left in Delft with whom to share ideas—and odd, crotchety Mijnheer van Leeuwenhoek, whose absorption in his lenses reduced the world rather than widening it. He must speak of everything in relation to what looking through them revealed.

But if Father dreamed of a different world, he did not say so. Indeed, he seemed quite content to bid the men goodbye and return to the world of his *View of Delft*. It had seemed a perfect world to me for some time now, but he was not yet satisfied with it. Lately, he had spent a great deal of time standing before the canvas, staring at it, brush in hand. I never knew exactly what he saw there that made him approach it and make some seemingly small change that, in fact, affected the composition profoundly. He had first painted the twin towers of the Rotterdam Gate in bright sunlight; then later recast them in shadow. He had extended the watery reflections of these towers downward, anchoring them to the opposite shore. Now he contoured the dark buildings in the foreground with a thin white line, defining them more visibly against the sky.

Outside, the air grew colder. Bitter winds came in from the sea, shook the last dry leaves from their branches, and sent them skittering on the cobblestones. Father laid on the glazes, oblivious; but I felt the weather's rages in my heart. I could not bear to look at the nearly finished painting, for I did not want this time with my father to end.

✛ ✛ ✛ ✛ ✛

When the last little changes Father had made to the painting were dry, Mijnheer van Ruijven's men came and swaddled the canvas in soft cloth, then took it to the framer. Soon afterwards, near the Feast of St. Nicolas, Father received word to come and view it in its place. I was invited to come along to visit with Mijnheer van Ruijven's daughter, Magdalena.

There was new snow on the ground when we set out, and the sky was leaden, promising more to come. Townspeople hurried along, huddled in their heavy wool cloaks. Skaters made circles on the ice that had formed on the Oude Delft Canal. Wind sleds flew past them, their sails flapping. I breathed deeply, despite the sharp unpleasantness of the cold rushing down into me, for I liked the way, when I breathed out, tiny white clouds formed and dissolved into the air. Was this how God made clouds, I wondered? It pleased me to think of Him breathing holy vapor out into the heavenly air, then stilling each puff with His hand and floating it down toward the earth to blot out the sun and so remind us how much we loved it.

Annetge, Mijnheer van Ruijven's maid, opened the door to us, and there was Father's painting in the front hall. It was so full of light that it warmed me. And even as I looked at it, I missed it as fiercely as I might have missed a much-loved person who had moved to a faraway land. Did Father feel the same way? I glanced at him, but nothing was revealed in his expression. Still I could not help wishing that the painting might be hung in Grandmother's house. If we could all wake every morning to its light, if we could live in that light, wouldn't we be happy?

I told myself to remember to be grateful to Mijnheer van Ruijven. But for his commission, the painting would not exist at all. If it had not been for his faith, Father must paint the dull things that others painted to earn enough guilders for our keep.

Soon he appeared, beaming, and shook Father's hand. "What do you think of your beautiful city, Jan? Is it not astonishing to walk in from the street and find yourself directly before it? I am quite certain I shall never open the door again without feeling for a moment as if it has provided a passageway to another world, instead of to the familiar surroundings of my own house. Even the smell of Annetge's baking from the kitchen cannot dispel it."

Father smiled. "It is good you are pleased."

We left our shoes in the front hall and followed Mijnheer van Ruijven into the drawing room, wearing the soft slippers that he kept in the front hall for his guests. The two men went to the chairs near the crackling fire and, preparing their pipes, began to talk.

This was my favorite room in the house, so rich, with its elegant carved fireplace and polished oak walls. Everything in it shone: the floors, the brass chandelier, the blue and white tiles lining the fireplace, the Delft plates propped on the mantel. Waiting for Magdalena to come, I wandered about, peering first through the green velvet curtains into the bed cupboard piled invitingly with blankets and pillows, then through the wavy panes of glass in the front window, to see the skaters outside on the canal. Father's painting of a girl sleeping hung on one wall. Just below it was a table with a thick Turkish rug on it, much like the one on the table in the painting. Today a white cloth covered most of the real rug, which meant that when Magdalena arrived, Annetge would bring us cakes and tarts on a silver tray.

My mouth watered at the thought of such special treats. I was glad to hear Magdalena's step on the stairs, then her voice directing Annetge to bring them. She bounced into the room in her usual merry way, her brown eyes sparkling. She was a pleasant, kind-hearted girl—as pretty as my sister, Maria. Prettier, I secretly thought. Today she wore a blue dress the color of the roofs in Father's *View of Delft*. Her brown hair curled out from under her blue velvet cap. She carried a doll dressed as prettily as she was.

"You may hold her, Carelina," she said.

I took her doll and held it as carefully as I had held our own baby,

Gretje, when she was newborn. Magdalena had offered it from kindness, I knew, believing that anyone who loved a dollhouse as much as I loved hers surely must love dolls as well. In fact, I did not care for them at all—and never had. But I feared she would find me too strange if I tried to explain that what I loved about her *poppenhuis* was simply the sight of it, the feel of its miniature objects in my hand and the endless ways in which I might arrange them.

We had our cakes and warm milk mixed with chocolate, Magdalena all the while chattering to me about a dozen different things: her harpsichord lessons, her uncle just home from the Indies with crates of marvelous things, the silver skates she felt certain St. Nicolas would bring her.

"I do think she wants me now," Magdalena said then, of her doll. So I handed it back and watched her tenderly press cake crumbs to its lips with her fingers. She had no brothers or sisters of her own. She could not know how willful real babies were, how they cried at the drop of a hat and made everyone cross who must listen to them.

Climbing the wide oak staircase, following her to her sleeping room where the *poppenhuis* was kept, I thought it must be wonderful to live as she did: just she and her father and mother in this lovely, quiet house. Were I Magdalena, I should never, ever want to leave. Just climbing that staircase seemed to me like climbing to heaven! There was a long, narrow, stained-glass window high above the landing, where the stairs turned to go to the second story, and I could not help but stop for a moment in delight amidst the pools of colored light that fell from it and patterned the floor.

"Carelina, come!" my friend called, and I hurried after her.

The *poppenhuis* sat on a table with thick legs carved to look like twisted rope. The house itself was as tall as a child, so I must stand on the three-step ladder Magdalena kept beside it to see the top story. There, tiny laundered linens hung from rods in the rafters just like our own linens hung in Grandmother's attic. There was a table with dry, laundered linens folded on it, ready for the tiny linen press. I stood on the ladder and looked at it, actually feeling the cold, damp air wet linens made, smelling the soap.

Who had made these things? Tiny chamber pots, foot warmers, bird cages, candles, baskets filled with balls of colored thread. A broom. Turkish rugs for the tables. Cupboards of Delftware. Pictures that must have been painted with a brush made of a single hair. A tiny mandolin!

The sleeping room was elegant: a bed, curtained in rich red fabric, tasseled in gold—fit for a tiny queen. The drawing room, too, with its carved fireplace and velvet chairs. In the kitchen, there were little painted tiles in the fireplace, copper cooking pots hanging from iron hooks. Pewter plates and tankards on the table. There was a tiny family, too: a father, mother, and daughter. No grandmother, no sisters or brothers, no crying babies needing to be comforted and fed.

I could not believe that Magdalena did not want to play with the *poppenhuis* every waking moment. But she would rather play with her dolls that were the size of real babies. There was a whole line of them on a shelf: each one with a beautifully painted face and real hair, each one beautifully dressed. She crooned to them, rocked them in a little cradle, sat them at the doll-sized table and served them meals on doll-sized crockery.

Today, thankfully, she was so busy with them that I had the *poppenhuis* to myself. In a corner of the drawing room, there was a round table which had, instead of legs, a single gold Cupid, arms raised, as its support. Carefully, so not to break them, I gathered some of my favorite things and arranged them on the surface. A porcelain jug shaped much like the one Father often painted, a pewter bowl with tiny apples in it, a brass candlestick, a sheet of music the size of my thumbnail. I set one of the chairs at a slant beside it, set the mandolin on the seat, then took the mandolin away and replaced it with folded linen. I lay the mandolin on the floor beside the Cupid, as if he had abandoned it to hold up the table. This pleased me so much that I wished to make a tiny picture of it in paint. I smiled to think of a paint brush small enough to fit the hand of a doll. Little paint pots and palette knives. I was sad to return the objects to their right places in the *poppenhuis* when Annetge came to tell me that I must go downstairs now, for Father was waiting.

The real house seemed so large as I walked through it to meet him. Outside, the people we passed on the street seemed to tower over me. I was frightened by the huge hooves of a workhorse that clopped by, pulling a sledge. I put my hand in Father's hand, kept my eyes to the cobblestones, and let him lead me home.

Snow began to fall hard that evening. Wind blew in from the sea, swirling the window glass with ice, so that it looked like the lens of one of Heer van Leeuwenhoek's microscopes swirled with stars. It grew bitterly cold. Tanneke fed the kitchen fire; and we gathered there, layered in our warmest clothing, our feet propped on foot warmers. Still, we shivered, chilled to the bone. And we children were afraid, for the wind seemed alive in its moaning, the creaking of the trees like doors opening to release captive spirits. Poor little Gretje sobbed in terror and could not be comforted, not even rocked in our mother's arms. Aleydis climbed on Father's lap and hid her face in his waistcoat. Grandmother was stern about such foolishness. She reprimanded Tanneke, who peered anxiously out of the windows and then bade us watch the flicker of the fire closely in case some omen were revealed in it.

"It is but a storm," Grandmother said. "Whatever is our Lord's will shall come of it." Still, she remained among us long after the time had passed when she would normally light a candle and climb the stairs to her bed chamber alone.

My eyelids grew heavy. I heard the bells of the Nieuwe Kerk chime ten and then eleven. Next time I heard them, they chimed twice, and I was tucked into bed with my sisters. The wind had ceased, and the small, familiar noises of the sleeping house asserted themselves upon my consciousness. The low crackle of the fire, a busy mouse inside the wall, my sisters breathing. I burrowed beneath the blankets, and my feet found the heated bricks that Tanneke had wrapped in flannel and placed in our bed. I was so warm, so perfectly content that I would likely have gone directly to sleep again with no more than a sigh, if the smell of tobacco had not told me that my father was still awake. I brought one hand out from the covers to part the bed curtain and shuddered, for the air was frigid.

Father seemed oblivious to the cold. Indeed, he was nowhere near the fire he'd stayed awake to tend, but stood before the drafty window, looking out. He breathed in the blue smoke of his pipe, breathed it out. He held a candle. When I raised up for a better view, I saw that the warmth of the flame had made a wet circle on the glass.

He turned then, and saw me. "It is cold *schaapje*," he said. "Best you stay snuggled there with your sisters."

But he did not forbid me to join him, and so I climbed out of my bed.

"Mother?" I asked.

"Sleeping. Everyone sleeps but you and me, Carelina. So it is ours, this beautiful new snow. Look at it."

I rose to my tiptoes so that I might see through the circle his candle made on the pane. Outside, the snow still fell. Earlier, the wind had chilled it into mean slivers of ice and driven it, slantwise, against the window. Now fat, lazy flakes drifted down, blurring the outlines of the houses, haloing the lit street lamps so that it looked as if a column of angels were marching toward us.

By morning, the world had become like one of Mijnheer van den Velde's cheerful winter landscapes. The tree limbs seemed neatly iced with white paint. Roofs and roadways seemed no more than white swaths made with the flat of a brush. The sky was porcelain blue, silver smoke curling into it from cozy brown houses. Brightly bundled skaters whizzed past on the canal, the blades of their skates winking in the sun.

I expected to find Father in his painting room, making use of the light. Indeed, it was a marvel to see. It streamed through the mullioned windows, softening the edges of everything it touched, rendering it golden and dreamlike. But the room was empty. I wandered the house looking for him, but he was nowhere to be found. Perhaps he has gone to Mechelen, I thought, to see if Grandma Digna had managed to keep warm throughout the night, if there was anything she needed.

I layered warm woolens over my dress, put on my mittens and slipped outdoors. Our neighbors in *Papenhoek* were out, digging and sweeping the snow from their doorsteps, and they greeted me with good cheer. I made my way across icy cobblestones through Great Markt Square to Mechelen, and found Grandma in the kitchen, kneading bread at the big wooden table, humming tunelessly—her bread song, I called it when I was a little girl. I surprised her with a quick hug, and her hands flew up, making a snowfall of flour on the floor.

She had survived the storm quite nicely, she told me. And Jutte had kindly gone out to run her errands. Her eyes twinkled when I asked if she had seen Father.

"He has been here, *schaapje*. If I were you, I should hurry back to your Grandmother Thins's house and see what he has gotten for you children."

"What—" I began.

But she touched a floury finger to my lips, and pushed me gently toward the door. "Go, now," she said. "He is in high spirits, and he will not want to wait long for you."

So I hurried back across the square; and the moment I turned onto Oude Langendijk, I saw him. He stood on the ice across from Grandmother Thins's house, beside a brightly painted sled: blue, with gold trim. Cornelia and the little ones gathered round him, clamoring for his attention. Tanneke stood on the front step, wiping her hands on her apron, beaming.

Aleydis ran to greet me, tugging at my hand. "Carelina," she said. "Come. We are to take a ride on the new sled Father has brought for us. And old Mevrouw van Best has lent her pushchair so Mother and Gretje can go along."

Indeed, as we approached, Maria and Elisabeth appeared with it; and, with Father's help, set it onto the ice: a wooden armchair, with curved metal runners attached to its legs and fitted with warm wool blankets. He made a signal to Tanneke, who brought Gretje out, bundled in woolens. Mother followed, wearing her yellow jacket with the ermine trim. Father settled her in the chair, drawing the blankets around her; then took Gretje from Tanneke and set her tenderly in Mother's arms.

Where was Grandmother? I wondered, glancing anxiously toward the window. I expected her to come out and scold me the moment I came into her view. Surely she had noted my absence and realized that I had set out without her permission.

"She is angry with Father," Cornelia whispered. "For buying the sled with the money from Mijnheer van Rujven. She went upstairs and closed her door when he came home with it. And she does not think it proper for Mother to go out in her condition."

If Father was aware of her disapproval, it was not apparent. He was as excited as a child himself, skating circles around his purchase, showing it proudly to our neighbors and to skaters who stopped to look. He greeted me warmly, then arranged us children on the sled, placing the little ones between me and Cornelia for safety. Tanneke brought us blankets, and warm bricks to hold in our hands. Father's dear friend, Mijnheer Samuel, stood nearby, puffing on his pipe. He had kindly agreed to pull us children; Father would push Mother and Gretje in the chair.

I believe that I have never been as happy as I was that winter morning, skimming through our town of Delft on the beautiful blue sled. Father and Mijnheer Samuel sang merrily as we went, in low booming voices. Mother laughed, Gretje crowed in delight. "Faster!" Aleydis called again and again, as if poor Mijnheer Samuel were a workhorse.

Skaters wound round us, as if in a dance. They flew past, bodies bent for speed, hands clasped behind their back; they spun, spraying ice chips that sparkled like diamonds in the sun; they snaked along in columns, each with his hands on the hips of the person in front him, leaning right, then left, in perfect time. Boys played crack the whip, sending one another sprawling. Rich burghers and their wives dressed in fur coats glided by, arm-in-arm. Up and down the canals we went, stopping now and then at the tents that innkeepers had set up at the side of the ice. We warmed ourselves at the fire, drank warm milk or cider flavored with cinnamon.

It was near dusk by the time we returned home, famished, to the smell of Tanneke's *hutespot* and baked bread. But for the kitchen, the house was dark. Grandmother would have her meal upstairs, Tanneke said. Father took a step toward the staircase, as if to bid her come and join us; but then stopped and took his place at the table. Mother sat beside him and we children gathered round, as well: a tired, happy family, a *poppenhuis* family, basking in the pleasure of a perfect day.

✣ ✣ ✣ ✣ ✣

It was soon afterwards that Gretje took ill. She sneezed; her eyes were red and streaming. Tanneke applied poultices to her chest and mixed herbal remedies to soothe her throat. She sprinkled vinegar round her bed to ward off infection and had her breathe in the vapor of sweet milk, which she said was known to be a cure for festering ears. Mother rocked and rocked her, but Gretje would not sleep.

By the Eve of St. Nicolas, we were all at our wits' end. Poor Gretje had awakened at dawn, crying, and was crying still. Bereft of our mother's attention, Beatrix sat and fiercely kicked the table leg. Maria teased Aleydis and made her cry. By midday, the squabbling and complaints escalated to such a great degree that Father was driven to disappear, claiming necessary business at the guild house; and, at his departure, Mother burst into tears.

Poor Tanneke looked a fright. Between baking the cookies and breads for tomorrow's feast day, cleaning the vegetables, and plucking and stuffing the chickens, she jiggled Gretje on her lap, clucked and crooned, trying to soothe her. But nothing made Gretje happy, not even the *flokker*, soaked in milk and sugar, that she usually loved to suck on. She squirmed and cried the whole time Tanneke dressed her for mass and pulled at the ribboned whalebone frame that held her head-cushion in place, as if the little helmet caused her pain.

Thankfully, the peaceful atmosphere of our beautiful secret church calmed us all. I loved climbing the winding stairs, up through the perfectly ordinary first and second stories where the Jesuits lived, to the long, narrow attic room that seemed like heaven. Everywhere you looked you saw something beautiful. The glistening white marble altar with gold candlestick holders and chalices set on embroidered altar clothes, silver organ pipes rising behind it. There were painted statues of Jesus and Mary, paintings of the saints in ornately carved frames, gold and silver reliquaries encrusted with gems that sparkled in the candlelight.

Tonight the church was decorated for the Feast of St. Nicolas; white candles twinkled all along the aisle and in the chandeliers. We sat in Grandmother Thins's special pew, all in our best clothing. Tanneke was with us, in her festival dress—a starched white linen tucker beneath a blue bodice, a red skirt bordered with black, and a dainty cap. She still smelled of the gingerbread she had been baking just before we left. She held Gretje, who seemed calmed by the beauty surrounding her. Or perhaps she had just grown too tired to cry. Still, she fought sleep. Her eyes closed, then flew open again; and she gave a cranky little moan.

Our poor mother was as tired as Gretje was, and worried as well. Her eyes closed, too; her head drooped to her chest. Then she sat up abruptly, glancing anxiously at Grandmother Thins to see if she had noticed. But Grandmother was praying, perhaps for Gretje's good health, and did not see. While the others of our parish entered and took their places, she knelt, her lips moving silently, the blue beads of her rosary slipping through her fingers.

I should pray, too, I thought. But I was cold and did not want to give up the comfort of my foot warmer to kneel as I must to pray properly, so I occupied myself watching the church fill up with our neighbors. Heer de Cocq, the apothecary, his wife and seven children, all in a row. Heer Samuels, the stonemason who had joined our winter excursion. The widow, Mevrouw van Best, who had lent Mother her chair. There was Grandmother's good friend, Heer de Coge; her cousins, the van Rosendaels. Mevrouw Huybrechts, the bookseller;

old Heer Bramer, one of Father's teachers when he was a boy. In the front pew sat Heer van der Velde and his family. He had been given that most honored place because he was such a help to the Jesuit brothers, even giving them one of his houses to live in.

I thought, as I often did, about how beautiful the vast spaces inside the Oude and Nieuwe Kerks must have been in that long-ago time when they belonged to us. I wondered how the Protestants, no matter what they believed, could have stood before the magnificently painted images of our Lord, bathed in the rich, luminous color of the stained glass windows, and then methodically set about to destroy them.

They feared beauty, Father said when I had asked him how this could have been. They feared imagining the face of God. They feared even the stories of the saints, and were forbidden by their church to celebrate their feast days. Still, I knew it was not only we Catholic children who left our shoes out, hoping for presents, on St. Nicolas Eve. Hadn't Magdalena van Ruijven had told me she was certain that St. Nicolas would leave her some silver skates? Hadn't he left the *poppenhuis* on her hearth last year?

What I did not understand was why, when Magdalena was not Catholic, the saint would leave her something so much grander than what he left for me. There would be candy and fruit in my shoes the next morning. Some ribbon for my hair. And probably a cloth doll, which I would pretend to play with for a few days and then give to Beatrix, who loved dolls as much as Magdalena did.

Father was the only one I would have dared asked why this was so, but I feared the question would make him sad for he would know, then, that I was discontent with what I was given. If I asked Grandmother, she would tell me it was sinful to doubt a saint's judgment, sinful to covet Magdalena's possessions. Mother did not like any question, no matter what it asked. I looked at her now, her face like an angel's, and I would not have troubled her for the world. Father was looking at her too, with an expression of concern. He took her hand in his, and she smiled up at him. When mass began, their two hands were still intertwined.

Father loved her so. He often told us children the story of how she had appeared one day with Grandmother in the studio of his master, Bloemaert, in Utrecht. Just one glance told him that he wanted very much for her to admire him, and he had blushed with gratitude when Mijnheer Bloemaert introduced him as his most gifted pupil. Then to learn that she resided in Delft—just across the Great Markt Square from Mechelen! It seemed a kind of promise to him, he said. He did not forget her, though a year passed before he saw her a second time—in Delft, strolling with her mother along Oude Langendyk. Nor had she forgotten him. He knew this because at the sight of him her face lit up in a smile. He knew, too, that he would not travel to Italy with Mijnheer van Hoogstraten as he had planned. He must court and win her. He must also win our grandmother's blessing.

He was poor, he was not Catholic. Mother was not strong. Grandmother Thins felt it might be best for her not to marry at all. She consented only after Mijnheer Bramer came to her in Father's behalf. He knew no young man of better character, he told her; and though his family was not rich, they were good people who had raised him well. "He will cherish your Catharina," he said.

The organ music swelled all around me and filled me with happiness so that I no longer cared about what I did not have. Our priest told the story of St. Nicolas. On either side of me, Aleydis and Beatrix shuddered when he described how three wealthy boys were robbed and murdered in the middle of the night by the landlord of an inn where they had stopped to rest. Then he cut their bodies into little pieces and threw them into a tub of brine, meaning to sell them as pickled pork! But St. Nicolas had a vision and, in it, saw what the landlord had done. He went directly to the inn and confronted the landlord, who fell to his knees, begging forgiveness. "Please bring the boys back to life," he said. And so St. Nicolas did. The boys jumped out from the brine tub, one by one, and cast themselves at his feet. Ever after, St. Nicolas had kept good Catholic children safe.

Later that night, we children set our shoes on the hearth and prayed to St. Nicolas to make our baby sister well. She had grown worse after church. Her breath was harsh. She was flushed with fever that did not abate, even when Tanneke held a cool cloth soaked in rose water and vinegar to her brow. She would not take her *flokker*, even soaked with brandy. Father called on Mijnheer de Cocq, though by then the hour was late, but the remedy Mijnheer de Cocq gave him did not help Gretje either. Near morning, he went next door to the priests' house and roused Father Jans.

This frightened me. My sisters lay, asleep and dreaming, around me; but I had not been able to sleep and for hours had watched quietly through a crack in the bed curtain. Now I pulled the curtain closed—as if to erase what I feared from my view might somehow diminish its power. I lay very still in the darkness, praying for sleep, half expecting Mother to cry out that St. Nicolas had come at last. There he would be on our hearth, in his beautiful embroidered robe, his jeweled gloves, his tall peaked hat. He would smile upon Gretje, raise his staff, and she would return to us as she had been, loving and cheerful. Surely he would come. On his day, would he not see that every sick child was spared?

I slept finally. In the morning, I woke to silence and crept out of my sleeping cupboard into the front room where my parents slept. When first I saw Gretje in her cradle, her little face looked so peaceful that I thought she slept, too. I thought our prayers had been answered. Then I looked again, and remembered that Gretje always slept curled up, like a kitten. Now she lay on her back, perfectly still, her little hands crossed on her chest. I touched one and drew back instantly. It was so cold. I shivered, suddenly cold myself. It was then that I heard Tanneke crying.

She was huddled on the hearth, near our empty shoes. "He did not come," she said. "He did not come. Your sister has gone to the Lord. Oh, your poor mother and father. God help them. She is gone."

Soon afterwards, Mother woke crying, and no one could console her, not even Father. He paced the room where Gretje lay, each time stopping short of her cradle. He could not bear to see her. I saw this from where I sat in the kitchen, as if through a frame, and could not help but imagine how my father might render it in paint. His own sad face; Grandmother, erect, in one of the lion's head chairs; Maria and Elizabeth, silent and pale. I might have helped Cornelia tend to the little ones, but I could not. I felt weightless, strange. My own hands, heavy in my lap, did not seem real to me.

Near me, Tanneke cried, preparing the sweet rice pudding that was always given to the children in a family when there had been a death. I did not want it. Nor did I want the cakes she had made to celebrate St. Nicolas Day. Poor little Beatrix clamored for them, though. And cried bitterly, but not from grief for our sister. Gretje was right there in her cradle. Why did we say she was gone? She cried because St. Nicolas had left her shoe empty.

"Was I not good, Father?" she asked, sobbing. "I tried very hard to be good."

I shall never forget the expression on his face when she said that: first, an almost ghostly smile, for the sweet absurdity of Beatrix's plea had brought with it a truth he had not seen before; then, gathering in his kind eyes, his own new truth, born of the morning's terrible sadness. He drew Beatrix to him, held her close a long time. Then he bent and whispered something in her ear.

"Carelina," he said. "Take Beatrix with you to the kitchen. There is something I must attend to."

Beatrix took my hand willingly. In the kitchen, Tanneke lifted her and held her close as Father had. She dressed her and fed her cakes for breakfast.

Soon I heard Father's step on the stairs, then he appeared in the kitchen with Beatrix's little shoe stuffed with presents. "See *dochterken*," he said. "St. Nicolas did not forget you."

There were pretty hair ribbons and candy in it, and a top which he helped her set to spinning. From his doublet he drew a little cloth doll, which made her smile. She sat on a low stool, singing to it. Tanneke cried again when she saw this, as if the doll were our own dead baby.

"Jan!" Grandmother said when she came upon the scene. She clutched her rosary beads in her hands, her eyes flashed with anger.

"It is St. Nicolas Day, Mother Thins," he said quietly. "The child is only three."

Grandmother started to speak, then turned away from us.

He sighed. "Come, Carelina," he said.

I followed him to his painting room, where on his table I saw the rest of the gifts St. Nicholas had forgotten: dolls, sweets, whistles, jump ropes. Sheet music for Maria, rolled up and tied with a yellow ribbon. A pretty leather catechism for Elisabeth, a flute for Cornelia, a whirligig for Aleydis. There were hair ribbons and pretty trinkets. A rattle for Gretje. Among these brightly colored objects sat an artist's palette. It was polished walnut, smaller than any palette I had seen before, the thumbhole too small for Father's thumb to fit in it. Without thinking, I reached to claim it. Then I drew back, chagrined.

Father picked it up. "Yes, *dochterken*," he said. "It is yours. Take it. I have made it to fit your hand."

And sliding my thumb into the hole, balancing the silky surface of the palette with my four fingertips, a bolt of joy sliced through my sadness, for even at that moment I knew what the gift meant.

The next morning, Father took me to his painting room and gestured toward an easel, where a small blank canvas was propped. He smiled then. "It is time for you to begin, little helper," he said. He took Heer Fabritius's goldfinch from where it hung the wall and set it before me.

It was his most beloved possession. Just a small picture: a single goldfinch chained to its wooden perch, but I had heard him say many times that in it was all any painter needed to know. I must copy the painting again and again, he told me, learning as I went. I must mix my own colors, come to know the drag of them on the canvas and how the quality of each changed, laid one against the other. He had done this himself, as a young man, he told me. In time, he had begun to feel as if Fabritius's hand were guiding his own, to see traces of the master's brushstroke in his own work.

"It will take a long, long while for you to paint a bird as fine as this little goldfinch," Father said. "But, for now, just look. Make yourself ready."

I looked until the bird dissolved into no more than shapes of color: its face a red-brown, rounded-off square capped in black, its nose made by no more than a light brown triangle surrounded on two sides by a lighter red-brown, and thrust forward by a black outline. The bright yellow in its wing was a thick, uneven stroke that at the same time leapt out and pinned my eye to it, causing me to only half see the bird's fuzzy gray breast, his gray-green perch with curved brass rails, the delicate looping chain that imprisoned him.

Downstairs, Grandmother fumed. Painting was unsuitable for a girl, she said when Father told her of his plan for me. How would I find a husband? She was scandalized when he said I would not need one, for what he taught me would allow me to make a living for myself. He mentioned Maria van Oosterwijck of our town, whose flower paintings were much admired as far away as France. And Judith Leyster, who was now gone to the Lord, but who had studied with the great master, Frans Hals, in Haarlem, and become a master herself. At this, Grandmother stood up, her morning meal untouched, took her rosary from her apron pocket and left the room to pray. She did not argue further, however; no doubt because she believed that I was so plain and clumsy that, even if I *were* to become a proper young lady, no one would want me for his wife.

I sat quietly, loathe to let Grandmother suspect that I did not wish to marry. I believed, then, that marriage meant I must take on the responsibilities of a household and give myself completely to my husband's needs. I had no desire to spend my life this way. And I should not miss having children: the never-ending burden of attentiveness they demanded. Indeed, I dreamed of a small house all my own, with a painting room like Father's in it. There, I would paint my whole life away and meet Saint Peter at the gates of heaven with the scent of pigments, oils, and varnishes still on my hands.

# The Music Lesson

I N THE next weeks, grief at losing little Gretje clung to our household like fog. But when I think of that brief time, what I remember is the way I felt, brush in hand, my father's eye upon me. Having finished *View of Delft* and not to begin Lord Huygens's commission until the new year, he gave me his complete attention, gently guiding me in my new work, telling me stories.

Of course, he must tell me of Fabritius, whose simple goldfinch became more elusive, more mysterious each time I put my brush to the canvas and tried to copy it.

He was a man as deceptively simple as his work, Father said. Known for having served his apprenticeship with the master, Rembrandt, he had come from Amsterdam to Delft, and had at once sought out the companionship of fellow painters at Mechelen, where he was received by most with a mixture of wariness and awe. Would he think himself superior to them?

This fear he quickly dispelled, proving himself respectful of the work he saw, curious to learn of the thoughts and techniques from which it was born, and generous with his own knowledge.

He believed that art was to be shared among those who loved it best, and Father cherished the friendship that sprung up between them. He learned from Fabritius's great knowledge of craft and, more importantly, learned from him the way each moment is lost as quickly as we hold out our hearts to it, how the artist gives his heart anyway and in so doing lives forever.

Father was but nineteen years when they met, fresh from his own apprenticeship in Gouda. Fabritius was nearly thirty. But he treated Father as an equal, and the two spent hours talking in the corner of the tavern, walking the streets of the town. He was small and wiry, with curly black hair framing his face, tumbling to his shoulders. He was not handsome. His self-portrait, which I had seen at the Guild House, flaunted his large, broad nose; his full lips suggested a pout. Indeed, you might not have liked him for those lips or for the set of his shoulders which showed no humility. But his eyes: dark and deep-set. Not sad, exactly. It was just that, looking at them, you knew he saw *everything*.

He had seen the goldfinch, and I wanted so much to know how he had made it real. Father had copied it himself, in the months after Fabritius's death—so grateful that his friend had left it in his keeping, and I thought perhaps he had discovered its secret.

"How did he *make* it?" I asked.

The question made him smile. "Fabritius used to speak to me of his master, Rembrandt," he said. "The great man's fascination with wealth and opulence, his love of rich fabrics and jewels. The choices he must make to keep his house, to keep his many patrons happy. My friend did not want this. The simplest things were of the greatest interest to him. Things others believed they'd seen until he painted them and showed them—" He gestured toward the goldfinch. "They had not seen at all. Look again, Carelina. See how the bird dissolves into color before your eyes. And light. You ask, how did he make it? I cannot say. I can but tell you what he said when I asked the same question: 'Color and light. This is what the whole world is made of.'"

"It is paint, yes," Father went on. "Patiently ground from the best pigments. It is years of one's hand holding the brush. Eyes that learn to see the way colors lay on a face or bird or silver pitcher, one against the other. But it is the small miracle that occurs in every true work that marries form and illusion to make it real.

"Ah," he said, reading my face. "Do not despair, little one. As it is for you, it was for Fabritius—and remains for your own father. Any painter dedicated to his craft must find balance in what he sees and knows and hopes to paint and his feeling that he cannot possibly accomplish it. And it should be so, for certainty does not invite the miracle."

He said this matter-of-factly, some might have said coldly. Yet I was relieved, for in his voice I heard approval for the question I had asked him, perhaps a hint of hope, too, that in time he might unearth traits in me that would tell him we were truly kindred spirits.

I was sad when the new year came and Father must turn to his own work, but grateful to once again be able to provide him help. Heer van Leeuwenhoek would be his model for *The Astronomer*, he had decided. Not only because it was known that Lord Huygens's son admired his work with the microscope, but because Father found the awkwardness of his friend's large, lanky body bent over its scientific tasks pleasing to the eye. Perhaps, too, that largeness seemed in keeping with the largeness of the heavens.

Grudgingly, Heer van Leeuwenhoek had agreed to sit for him, though he insisted it must be in his laboratory at the back of his house. Secretly, I was glad, for it meant hours away from Grandmother's house. It made me think of the happy times with Father last summer, while he was painting his *View of Delft*.

Not that van Leeuwenhoek's laboratory was anywhere near as peaceful as that quiet room above the harbor had been. Indeed, his household was far more chaotic than our own, for Heer van Leeuwenhoek had five children and no wife to oversee them. She had died in childbirth some years ago, leaving the care of the house and the children—and often the drapery shop as well—to their eldest daughter, Maria. She was just a year older than I; but, sullen and trapped, she spurned any gesture of friendship I offered. She was jealous of the way her father had always indulged my curiosity about his lenses, I supposed; jealous of my own father's kindness toward me. Heer van Leeuwenhoek treated her harshly, demanding her services instantly upon his call, no matter what other task she was engaged in. She retaliated by allowing the little ones to run screaming through the house, by letting the dust pile up disgracefully in the corners.

Had Grandmother any idea of the state of their household, she certainly would have forbidden Father to take me there. Fortunately, her disdain for Heer van Leeuwenhoek was so great that she did her best to ignore his existence, and so knew only the least of his offenses. Perhaps, too, her greediness at the good news of Lord Huygen's large commission permitted her to overlook what she might otherwise have felt compelled to control.

Or maybe she did not care at all about me. Perhaps, finally, I had become invisible to her. She said nothing to me when I returned home with Father every day, nothing about the fact that I disappeared each evening to the painting room, where I lost myself in the gold-finch's light and shadow.

In any case, I accompanied Father to the laboratory each day and watched the painting of Heer van Leeuwenhoek take shape, much as I would have listened to a story. In the beginning, there was the simple delight in wondering what might come next, and then, as the painting developed, that same delight combined with a kind of inevitability that brought an even deeper pleasure.

First Father set about making a quiet corner in the cluttered room. Under Heer van Leeuwenhoek's anxious supervision, I helped clear an old table of the subjects and instruments of his studies—and sometimes sketched them on bits of paper he had abandoned. Glasses and beakers overflowed with seeds, feathers, fish scales, grains of sand. The papery outside layer of a tulip bulb, a hairball coughed up by his cat. There were mysterious substances, as well, which Heer van Leeuwenhoek identified as mosquito wings, legs of lice, flakes of his own skin—barely visible, which he had scraped onto a glass plate to examine.

Like Mijnheer van Hoogstraaten, he was fascinated with eyes, and his collection included the eyes of insects, dried mucous scraped from the eye of a beached whale, and a slice of the eye of a dead dog that he had found in an alley. He would not hesitate to slice a man's eye and study it, he told Father—should a surgeon be kind enough to give him one from a cadaver. I shuddered to hear him say this, though I could not help but wonder what such a study would reveal. In fact, I could not help but wonder about almost everything, and when Heer van Leeuwenhoek leapt up as he was wont to do, and retrieved some treasure from his cabinet of microscopes, I felt my heart quicken with excitement at the same time I knew the distraction would slow Father's progress.

But his patience was equal to Heer van Leeuwenhoek's impatience—the two of them as different as earth and sky, and he perused his own collection of objects with complete concentration. He left Heer van Leeuwenhoek's tall narrow cabinet in the corner of the room, a stair-step of books shelved on top. On the front of it, up high, he tacked an astronomical chart. In the far corner of the newly empty table, which he had set beneath the window, he placed a celestial globe. At its base, an astrolobe—half of it visible, face-up, between the globe and the blue and green tapestry he had draped at the forefront. A pair of dividers, some books. A volume of Metius open to "On the Investigation of the Stars."

He bade Heer van Leeuwenhoek to pull back his long brown hair and tuck it behind his ears in the manner of a scholar. He dressed him in a green robe, the color of the living world, then played at arranging him before the table much as I had arranged the objects in Magdalena van Ruijven's *poppenhuis*. First this way, then that; and all the while, Heer van Leeuwenhoek complaining. Finally, Father was satisfied. Heer van Leeuwenhoek leaned forward on his chair, the fingers of his right hand spread, touching the upper surface of the globe. His left hand lightly gripped the edge of the table.

Of course, he could not sit quietly while Father painted him. Against the thuds and shouts of children playing, the regular appearance of Maria at the doorway with some concern, he spoke of many things—most often, the ideas of Spinoza, an excellent lensmaker like himself, and a philosopher, too.

They had met during Heer van Leeuwenhoek's travels as a young man, and perhaps it was because he was so impressed by Heer Spinoza's depth of knowledge about lenses that he was so troubled by his ideas about God.

God was not a separate entity, Spinoza said. He did not create the world to stand outside it. He *was* the world: all of nature, every living being. He could not, then, be the father that mankind imagined Him to be. How could He be a father, when He was everything? When everything was Him?

What were *we* then? Ourselves, yes; and, at the same time, part of the larger thing, which was God, Himself. As for the devil, Spinoza did not believe in him. If God was everything, then He must be the devil, too; or the devil, Him. Which simply was not possible.

Grandmother said these ideas were blasphemous, and would not allow Spinoza's name to be spoken in her house, let alone hear his beliefs discussed there. Perhaps in this she was right, for sometimes what I heard frightened me. But as I went about my work, preparing Father's paints and palettes, cleaning his brushes, sometimes sketching things around me, I could not help but listen.

"I believe as Descartes does," Mijnheer van Leeuwenhoek declared one day. "Reason is the path to knowledge, and science proves the world is knowable. God's world is a machine, which needs only to be seen to be understood. But one dare not trust his own senses," he warned. "For do not our dreams seem perfectly real when we are dreaming them?"

He set a grain of wheat on the tip of his finger and bade Father look at it, then me. Then he retrieved one of his microscopes from the cabinet. It was made of two oblong plates, several inches across and long, with one of Mijnheer van Leeuwenhoek's minute, hand-ground lenses clamped between them. Mijnheer van Leeuwenhoek fixed the grain of wheat on the lens with a pin. Father held the microscope to his eye and looked through it. Then Mijnheer van Leeuwenhoek bade me look, too. I glanced at Father, who nodded his permission.

I looked, and saw what looked like a lemon.

"It is a grain of wheat you see there, Carelina," Heer van Leeuwenhoek said. "If your naked eye could not see the true character of something so common, how could it see something as large and complex as God must be?"

The question frightened me, and I did not try to answer. But it seemed that this was the response Mijnheer wanted, for he smiled a small, satisfied smile, and told Father and me to look at the tower of the Niewue Kerk framed in the laboratory window. When we had done so, he retrieved another microscope from the cabinet, this one with a dragonfly's eye suspended beneath the lens.

"Hold it up to the window," he said. "Look at the tower through it."

Astonished, I saw as a dragonfly sees: multitudes of tiny, upside-down towers—each one no bigger than the point of a pin.

"So then," Mijnheer van Leeuwenhoek said, when each of us had

had our turn. "Does this make you doubt your eye even further? You see, Carelina," he went on, "doubt is the necessary starting point for all knowing. And—" His voice was triumphant. "Our knowledge of this one certainty yields the first absolute truth: one doubts. If one doubts, he must be thinking. If he is thinking, he must be a thinking being. Therefore, he exists. And if, existing, his mind holds in it the idea of a perfect entity, then that perfect entity—God—must exist, for the idea of a perfect entity could not have originated from an imperfect being.

"Descartes is clearly right in his thinking," Mijnheer van Leeuwenhoek concluded. "A perfect God would not deceive us. The world exists and was made by His hand, because we perceive this to be so with the reason He provided us. Thus, in time, the world shall be understood."

Father paused in his work, brush raised. "The world, perhaps," he said. "It is true that we can observe it. But our minds? How can we observe what we are observing *with*? And how can we understand the world made to house us, if we cannot understand ourselves?"

Mijnher van Leeuwenhoek sputtered, attempting a response.

But Father went on, his voice quiet and sure. "What we see, what the dragonfly sees: it is all real, my friend. And therein lies God's great mystery, proof that none of us can ever truly understand Him."

✢ ✢ ✢ ✢ ✢

I confessed the sin of questioning the essence of God to Father Jans, and obediently recited the Hail Marys he gave me for penance. Father knelt with his rosary when he left the confession booth, too. Had he asked forgiveness for the same sin? I could not imagine it, for during those conversations with Heer van Leeuwenhoek he spoke his thoughts with such passion. How could he regret them? Indeed, sometimes when we were walking home together he pondered aloud various points of their discussions with obvious pleasure. Perhaps this was his confession then: that he had allowed blasphemous ideas to be planted in my head.

Or perhaps it was not about ideas at all. Perhaps Father confessed that he had not given our mother the attention she craved during her difficult confinement. As the birth of the baby drew near, she had grown fretful and petulant. Despite Father's patient explanation that he must finish Lord Huygens's commission on time, she wept every morning when he left for Heer van Leeuwenhoek's laboratory. Why must he go, when she was so uncomfortable and in such poor spirits, still grieving for the loss of Gretje?

In truth, Father was consumed by *The Astronomer*. It was as if he himself were living somewhere in the stars. If he had meant to continue teaching me, he had forgotten it. Nor did he seem to notice that I spent stolen moments in the painting room, copying and recopying Fabritius's goldfinch. He was distant, even from our mother. If some urgency in her voice finally caught his attention, he turned to her, confused, and it took him a long moment to register her complaint. Evenings, he would bid Cornelia play something on the virginal to please us all. But he paced while she played, and clearly did not enjoy it.

When Tanneke lit the lamps, he commenced with our lessons, as usual; but he was easily distracted, rifling through books, poring over maps and charts he rolled out on the kitchen table. He spun Grandmother's globe, his fingertip traveling across blue oceans, pink and yellow continents. When the earth could no longer hold his interest, he gathered us children outdoors and taught us about the sky.

Above us, the moon shone yellow, like a wheel of cheese. It moved in unending circles around the earth, Father told us, as the earth moved in unending circles around the sun. Indeed, we were—all of us—spinning around the sun that very moment. This frightened me badly; and I took hold of Cornelia's hand, as if doing so might keep me from flying up into the heavens.

Next, thankfully, Father directed our eyes to the North Star, which the ancient navigators depended upon, for it remained fixed in the sky. It was also the first star in the handle of the Little Dipper, he said. And in the long tail of the Little Bear. Nearby were the seven bright stars that formed the Big Dipper and the Great Bear. You must look closely to see these patterns, Father told us, tracing the line of stars with his fingertip. The sky was full of pictures, each one with a story. The Great Bear, legend said, was once a beautiful girl who had been changed into a bear and placed in the sky by Zeus's jealous wife. Orion was a hunter loved by the goddess, Diana, and shot by her arrow. I loved the story of Pegasus, a winged horse that set out to carry Bellaphon to Mount Olympus. Stung by Zeus's gadfly, he bucked, and the poor boy plummeted to earth, where he wandered for the rest of his days, lame and blind.

My head was full of pictures, and after I had helped Cornelia put the little ones to bed, I walked up the stairs to Father's painting room. The latest of my goldfinches shone in the moonlight, a sorry thing. I might have tried again if Father had remembered to replenish the supplies he had given me. I might have sketched, but there was no paper in the room for Father sketched in paint on canvas. He did not draw, nor did he seem to have noticed that I had begun to draw. Indeed, I grew more and more fascinated with the way I had to look to replicate what I saw before me. I could not look at the *thing* at all, only the lines of it. Of course, my crayon could not capture the shine or texture of what I drew, as Father did with color. Still, it pleased me the way, line by line, a jug, a face, a tree emerged beneath my hand.

Later that night, after the bells had chimed midnight, I heard

Father creep through the kitchen and out the door into the frosty garden, where he stood so still for so long, looking up at the heavens, that I should have had time to draw a good likeness of him if I had had paper and a crayon at my disposal.

Instead, I drew him from memory the next morning, while he painted. I must only close my eyes and I could see him, his arms crossed on his chest, his head tilted up. I sat, tucked away in a corner, sketching, half-listening to Father and Heer van Leeuwenhoek debate the merits of art versus science.

It was science that mattered, Heer van Leeuwenhoek proclaimed. The measurable universe. Anything else was a matter of indulgence.

To Father, there was no real difference. "Doesn't painting accomplish essentially the same thing as you accomplish with your microscopes?" he asked. "To make a picture of the world, piece by tiny piece? What does a mapmaker do, but see the world and make a picture of it? What does an astronomer do, but see the stars and planets and draw them in their course?"

"Absurd," Heer van Leeuwenhoek said. "What you paint is not real."

But it was real. By then, the painting was finished, but for the last touches, and Father asked him to come and look at the canvas. Heer van Leeuwenhoek could not help but reach out to touch the globe painted there. Then he pulled his hand back and gazed upon it with an odd expression, as if surprised that the globe had not curved beneath his finger.

Father laughed. He was not the kind to press an argument once it was won.

All the while, I sketched him as he had been the night before. It was a good sketch, too. Had Cornelia not come just then to fetch us home, I likely would have shown it to him. But Mother's labor had started, and Father must go immediately to attend her.

93

When we arrived, Tanneke went for the midwife, informing neighbor ladies along the way. They hurried to gather in our kitchen, and stayed into the evening, gossiping, eating Tanneke's cakes, praying that this time the Lord might give our father a son. Occasionally, one would rise and enter the front room; then return, assuring the others that everything was proceeding as it should. The linen warmer was placed near the fire, the birthing chair near Mother's bed, the midwife's instruments laid out on a table. Tanneke kept the candles around Mother burning with a blue flame, to keep evil spirits from hovering near. She had made the cradle ready, covered its bedclothes with the special satin quilt under which each of us children had lain on our birth day. At its foot she placed clothes for the new baby: the embroidered baptism costume we had all worn, and everyday clothes, too.

After the neighbors left, we girls lay, restless, in our sleeping cupboard. We slept head-to-toe, Maria, Elisabeth, and Aleydis at one end; Cornelia, Beatrix, and I at the other. Our pillows were plumped so high, we were nearly sitting. Tanneke insisted on this. To lie flat, she said, invited the devil to come and sit on one's chest. But poor Beatrix was so small that she was virtually upright in the bed, and every night she twisted and turned, whimpering, before finally sleeping.

Tonight she was even worse than usual. It was quiet, just the low murmur of voices in the front room and Tanneke's occasional scuffling in the kitchen, following some direction the midwife had given. But perhaps Beatrix sensed that something was afoot. Little ones were still close to the spirit world, Tanneke always said. Perhaps Beatrix sensed something we older ones could not.

It frightened me to think that. What if it were the devil causing

Beatrix's unrest? What if he were here among us right now, waiting to snatch the new baby's soul? Or, worse, our mother's? And, the devil aside, Mother might die from the pain of childbirth alone. I had known children whose mothers died bearing them, or bearing a sister or brother, and they were always sad, lost, needy children. Oh, how would we live without our beautiful mother? How would Father live without her? Tears sprang to my eyes at the thought, and I drew Beatrix to me, rubbed her little back to comfort her, though, truth be told, I was the one comforted by our closeness. Mother would not die, I told myself. She would not.

"What if Gretje comes for the new baby?" Aleydis whispered. "What if she is lonely in heaven?"

"Hush," I said. "She won't come. She wants us to be happy."

"Even the highest angel cannot come back to earth unless the Lord allows it," Elisabeth said. "So if she does come to take the new baby, it is His will." She said this importantly, without emotion; but a moment later, I heard the clicking of her rosary beads and knew she had brought her rosary to bed with her to pray that He would keep Mother and the new baby with us.

It was a long, difficult birth. Mother moaned unceasingly. Several times, we heard her cry out. I was the one closest to the bed curtain, and I moved it slightly, so that I could see a slice of the empty kitchen if I held my head just right. The kitchen fire flickered, casting dancing shadows on the wall. Tanneke appeared now and then to tend to it, and to replenish the warm wine and broth meant to fortify Mother throughout her ordeal. She lay abed in the front room, attended by the midwife and Grandmother Thins. Father sat with her.

In time, my sisters drifted off to sleep around me. I heard the church clock chime midnight, one, two. Just after three o'clock, I heard the midwife send Father away; and, peeking through the curtain, I saw him enter the kitchen. He sat down at the table, put his head in his hands. With my own hands, I covered my ears. But I could hear still Mother moaning.

Thankfully, it was not long until I heard the baby's thin cry and a sound from Mother that sounded almost like laughter. Father stood, awaiting the midwife, and soon she came. Beaming, she put the new baby, swaddled in a blanket, in his arms.

"Here is your son," she said. "May our Lord grant you much happiness through him, else may He call him back to Him soon."

"A son?" he said. "A *son*."

And my heart cracked at his visible joy.

✣ ✣ ✣ ✣ ✣

In the morning, Tanneke made a caudle of ale mixed with sugar, eggs, bread, and spices. She stirred it with a long stick of cinnamon adorned with ribbons. She posted the *kraam kloppertje* on our front door. Made of paper and lace, it announced to the town that a male child had been born in our household.

Father donned the paternity bonnet and, ribbons flapping, he carried the tightly swaddled baby through the house, introducing him to our family and friends, who had arrived to celebrate little Johannes's birth. Grandma Digna, flushed and smiling. Old Heer Bramer. Heer de Cocq and his wife. Heer van Leeuwenhoek, who bent to peer at the baby through his smudged spectacles.

"See here, my son," Father said, "your grandmother's cousins, the Mejuffrouws Aleydis and Cornelia van Rosendael. And the fine baker, Heer van Buyten, who will give you a biscuit as soon as you grow some teeth to eat it with." To Magdalena van Ruijven, who came with her father, he said in all seriousness, "We found him beneath a cabbage leaf." And I saw that, having no brothers or sisters of her own, she believed him.

We children sat as near to Mother on the nursing chaise as we could. Her face as serene and beautiful as Father had painted it, she watched him with the new baby and received congratulations from our visitors. But, left alone for a moment, her eyes would flutter closed, revealing threads of blue vein on her eyelids. Tanneke and Grandmother fussed at the sight of this, begging her to restore her energies with the cheese and buttered bread and ewe's milk they had brought her. But she ate and drank only to quiet them. Once they turned away from her, she set the cup and plate back on the table beside her. Later, when everyone had gone home, she slept.

In the next days, Father would not let little Johannes out of his sight. Mother must nurse him, of course, but Father was the one to comfort him when he cried. At night, I could hear him pacing through the house, talking to Johannes, naming things—as if Johannes were already able to understand what the world was.

"Here, my son: a window." I heard a tap-tap on the glass. "And moonlight outside it. This, a table. A water jug. A chair."

He had done so with my younger sisters, too. I remembered it. No doubt, with Maria and me, as well. But my heart was bitter. Mornings, I crept up into Father's painting room and sat, alone, in the exact place where Mother had stood with the scales, and thought how, in time, the balance of Father's affection would surely shift to this beloved son. Johannes would become his apprentice, and I would be forgotten by him.

The table Father had painted was still beneath the window, with the jewelry boxes, the gold chain, the strings of pearls, the rumpled blue cloth still upon it. I half-expected to look up and see the *Last Judgment* hung on the wall. But, of course, Father had only imagined the painting, so the wall was blank.

Nonetheless, I felt the presence of our Lord judging me. I prayed with my rosary, asking His help. In the darkness of the confession booth, I whispered, "Father, I have sinned. I do not love my own brother." I did penance as Father Jans directed, but it brought me no comfort.

At the flurry of parties marking the first week of Johannes's birth, I was sullen and did not speak, incurring Grandmother's displeasure. I was cross with Cornelia, my favorite sister, and made her cry. And when I bunched my embroidery thread so badly that I must be given a fresh piece of linen, I did not say I was sorry.

When I could not bear the sight or sound of my new brother one more moment, I went outdoors and walked toward Great Markt Square all alone, which Grandmother had forbidden any of us to do. It was a raw, wet day in March and, crossing Oude Langendyk, I stopped and stood nearer to the thawing canal than I should, peered into the deep water, thinking how sorry Father would be if I were to fall in and drown. I imagined Father weeping as he looked upon my poor, swollen body, blue with cold. How he would wish, then, that he had paid me some attention!

I kicked a pebble hard and it pinged on an iron post. Were I a boy, like Johannes, I should be happier, I thought. Boys must not be pretty and good, only brave and clever. They must not stay inside and worry dust from every corner when there was a whole world full of wondrous things to see.

A girl could not even run away. Where would she go?

Resigned, I turned to go back to Grandmother's house, and that was when I saw Father hurrying toward me. His anxious expression made me fear that something terrible had happened. Then he reached me, knelt down beside me, and I saw that I was the one who had caused his distress.

I was sorry then, and looked away. But he turned me gently toward him, took my face in his hands. "Oh, my Carelina," he said. "*Dochterken*. Come."

I thought he would take me home, where Grandmother would scold me for worrying our poor mother. Instead, he took my hand and we started across the square.

"I have told Mother Thins that it is time we get back to work, you and I." He smiled. "I said we had urgent business at the Guild that might take us the better part of the morning."

But we passed the bridge to the Voldersgracht, which would have taken us to the Guild House, and my heart quickened, for I knew then that he meant to take me to Mechelen, to see Grandma Digna.

She was in the kitchen, chopping vegetables for a *hutsepot* when we arrived, and turned towards us at the sound of Father's voice. "Jan!" she cried. "And my own Carelina. Tell me what brings you. The little one, he is well?"

"Yes, well," Father said. "Though demanding for such a small fellow. Is it not so, Carelina?" He put his hand on my shoulder. "Are we not both up to our ears in babies and in need of some special attention? Mother, what do you have for us? Something sweet and good."

To my surprise, I felt my eyes fill up with tears, and I must look down at the floor to hide them. But Father knew. He sat down on a chair, pulled me to his lap, as if I were a small child, instead of nearly eleven. Grandma Digna bustled about us, setting almond paste cookies and beautiful fruit tarts on the table. Then, while we ate, she and Father told me the family stories I loved to hear.

✣ ✣ ✣ ✣ ✣

I wished, as I often did, that I might have known our grandfather. Father had hung his portrait, and Grandma Digna's, in the great hall at Grandmother Thins's house, and sometimes I stood and stared at them. The portraits had been made at the time of their marriage;

nonetheless, I could see Grandma Digna in the young woman who smiled back at me. When I looked at Grandfather, I saw Father. And myself. Our pale skin, our brown hair; our high forehead, wide-set eyes, and thin lips.

He had been trained as a caffa worker, and Father's earliest memories were of this rich, silk cloth still on the loom. He had loved to accompany his father to the workshops of his friends in the Small-Cattle Market, where Grandfather had lived and worked before establishing his first inn, the Flying Fox, on the Voldersgracht. Grandma Digna remembered how Father had collected the snipped threads of silk that had fallen to the floor beneath the men's looms, put them in his pocket, and carried them home, where he would lay them out on an unattended table in the inn and occupy himself arranging them in colorful patterns that pleased him.

"You are like him, Carelina," Grandma smiled. "I have seen you in the kitchen arranging the vegetables just so, holding the pewter pitcher up to catch the light. And you are devoted to him as he was devoted to his own father."

He had followed Grandfather everywhere, like a shadow, she told me. This, she believed, was why Father had always found himself at ease with so many kinds of people. Grandfather had been a gregarious man, who attended to the needs of the artists and businessmen frequenting his inn. At the same time, he remained involved in the lives of his friends from an earlier time and his relatives, many of whom were known to have been involved in dealings that were certainly odd, and sometimes illegal. His own mother, Neeltge Goris, had been accused of cheating a traveling merchant of some two thousand guilders, when she failed to fulfill a promise she had made to secure permission for a lottery from the Delft magistrates and then to arrange it. His brother-in-law had been imprisoned for counterfeiting.

Once, Father said, when Grandfather was a young man, he had had to flee Delft after severely wounding a soldier in a knife fight and could not return until Grandma Digna gave over six guilders as compensation for the man's pain and suffering, and paid the surgeon's bills, as well. This, I knew was a true story, for Grandma Digna giggled like a girl whenever Father told it.

Tears always filled her eyes when she spoke of how, as a little boy, Father had gazed hour upon hour at the pictures that the painters from the St. Luke's Guild brought to the tavern for our grandfather to sell. How, wreathed in the smoke from their clay pipes, he sat and listened to the men talk. One day, she said, Mijnheer van Aelst lifted Father to his knee and quickly sketched the features of one of the tavern maids on the rough wood table with a piece of chalk. Then, laughing, he handed the chalk to Father, who without hesitation sketched a perfect copy next to it. How astonished the men were, Grandmother said, for Father was only seven. They called our grandfather to see. And herself. And our Aunt Gertruy. Mijnheer van Aelst was often in debt to Grandfather, and it was decided that, to earn his food and drink, he would teach Father until it was time for him to be apprenticed. And so he had.

I loved the sound of Grandma's voice; I loved these old familiar stories; and, listening, I drifted backward to the time, long ago, when we had lived with her at Mechelen. Our family was smaller then: just Father, Mother, Maria, and me.

We were happy there. But Grandmother Thins convinced our mother that we must move to her house in Papists' Corner, or God would punish her for raising us children in a tavern, where we were tempted daily by sinful, uncatholic ways. Grandma Digna never spoke of these things when I came to visit her, just opened her arms and drew me in so joyfully that I knew she longed for our return.

I, too, longed for it! Head bent, ashamed, I whispered this longing to Father Jans in the confession booth. Afterwards, I knelt and prayed to the blessed Mother Mary for strength, as he had instructed me to do. I prayed to be grateful for what Grandmother Thins provided us: warm beds, good food, and a right relation to God. For her devotion to our mother, who was kind and beautiful, but not strong. I prayed He might grant all our hearts entry to the tranquil Delft that Father had painted in the room above the harbor.

As if angry that the formal celebration of his birth had come to an end, Johannes began to cry—and did not stop. He cried throughout the day, cried himself to sleep, and woke, crying, nearly every hour through the night. Every morning, Father fled to Mijnheer van Louewenhoek's to finish the painting and prepare it to be sent to Lord Huygens, but I must stay to help Cornelia with the little ones.

Fearing there was something wrong with Mother's milk, Tanneke bid her drink brown ale and eat stewed vegetables and sour fruits. But Mother could not eat, and as she grew weaker, her milk left altogether.

A wet nurse must be engaged, which brought Mother's spirits even lower. Terrible stories about wet nurses abounded: one fell asleep by the fire while nursing, and the baby fell from her arms and was burned; another, in a drunken stupor, drowned her charge while bathing him. We were fortunate to find a sweet, quiet girl from Tanneke's village, so we need not worry that she would harm Johannes, or that bad traits would be passed to him through her milk. Still, a mother's milk was blood that had whitened in the breast, the same blood that had nourished the infant in the womb and to which it had grown accustomed. So while our brother was nourished by Susana's milk, it was little comfort to him. Still he cried, and Mother could not bear to turn away from him, even when Father said that at times little Johannes's willfulness put him in mind of our Uncle Willem.

This worried me, for I did not want anyone else like Uncle Willem in our lives. He had become more menacing after the day he threatened Mother with the stick. More than once, he humiliated Mother and Grandmother, shouting obscenities at them in the town square; often he stood before our house and shared his grievances against them with any passerby who would listen. Then shortly before Johannes's birth, I was on my way on an errand for Tanneke and he appeared before me, as if from nowhere. He grasped my shoulder so roughly that he left bruises and bade me tell our grandmother to allow him his birthright or else he would take one of us instead. This finally convinced the regents of Delft that he was a danger to our family, and he was confined to Heer Taerling's house of correction.

This had brought us all relief. Now the fierceness with which little Johannes continued to assert his will made us uneasy again and added to the atmosphere of tension that the presence of our growing family caused in Grandmother's house.

As if it could calm us, Father painted music. Full of color and light, a perfect geometry in the black and white marble floors and in the arrangements of figures and musical instruments, the paintings he made during the year after Johannes's birth were so beautiful and real that, looking at them, I felt the same comfort and joy that listening to music had always made me feel, and I was grateful to be allowed to help him.

The window from which the light entered, the white porcelain jug, the chair with the lions' heads, the red and gold and blue Turkish carpet: the variation of these and other elements from one painting to the next seemed to me a visual counterpart to the pleasurable variation of a simple musical phrase. Perhaps of all Father's paintings, I loved these best. The expression I saw on his face while he made them was the same expression that I had seen on his face and on our mother's when, in happier times, they had spent whole evenings playing music together.

Music had been her first love. Grandmother bought a virginal when they moved from Gouda to Delft, and it was both the concentration that it took our mother to master the keyboard and the delicate, soothing sounds of the instrument itself that finally delivered her from the fear and unhappiness of her childhood. But Grandmother had intended music lessons to be just one aspect of Mother's education as a young lady. She was not pleased when Mother became possessed by the music, lost herself in it for hours at a time. She would not learn needlework, would not learn what she must know if she were to manage a household someday. She would not socialize with the young ladies and young men of the town whom Grandmother deemed proper companions. She would only play and sing.

And though she had been drawn to Father's kind face the first time she saw him at work in Heer Bloemart's studio, it was music that had made her fall in love with him; for there was no musical instrument that he could not master, no musical composition that he could not play by ear after having listened to it once or twice. The lute, the viol, the trombone: our grandfather had played all these instruments, and others that had once belonged to his stepfather. Thus, there had been music in Father's life as long as he could remember and ample opportunity for him to develop into a musician in his own right. As a boy, living at Mechelen, he had been a favorite of the tavern's patrons, accompanying the musicians who played and sang for their pleasure.

I remembered musical evenings at Mechelen myself: Mother at the virginal, Father accompanying her on the bass viol. Maria and I were allowed to stay up far past our usual bedtime, listening to our parents make music together; and, even now, if I closed my eyes, I could feel myself gathered in Grandma Digna's arms, drowsy against her soft bosom. I could feel the music enter me with each breath I took and circulate throughout my body, as much a part of me as my own blood.

Even after we came to live with Grandmother Thins, Mother and Father played and sang together, though they had not done so since Gretje's death. Lately when Father played, it was most often with Cornelia. Maria was the older and more proficient, but Cornelia played with a passion that he enjoyed. She had his ear for music as well, and delighted in mimicking what she heard him play, creating tuneful variations with her nimble fingers.

And I believe that when she stood at the virginal, her hands poised above the keys in that moment just before she began to play, Father sensed in her the same feeling he had when he stood before a blank canvas, his brush still heavy with the promise of its first stroke.

I was glad for his appreciation of her. Cornelia was steady and loyal, with a desire to please that both endeared me to her and made me sad, for in her earnest efforts she was so often disdained by our grandmother. In the late morning, when my time with Father was through, I would often find her in a corner of the kitchen playing quietly with the little ones while Tanneke set our midday meal on the table. She had endless patience with their games. She spun Aleydis's top, helped Beatrix dress and undress her dolls, built towers with Johannes's wooden blocks so that he might knock them down. Neighbor children would call to her to come jump rope or play Blind Man's Bluff. But Cornelia would smile and decline. In the afternoons, when the little ones were banished to the outdoors so that our mother might rest, she watched over them and made certain they were safe. I sat beneath a linden tree, distracted by the visions in my own head, longing for a time when my father might again teach me.

In the year that Father painted music, there were not only the troubles of our own family to consider, but the troubles of our Dutch nation, for we had gone to war against England. It had begun with a sea battle off Lowestoft—the fighting so fierce that it was said the blast of the guns could be heard as far off as The Hague. Seventeen of our warships were sunk or captured, causing considerable distress among the townspeople of Delft, who feared that, so sadly depleted, our navy had little chance of holding its own. But more immediate than the danger of invasion was the effect the war had on the finances of a country almost completely dependent upon foreign trade. Grandmother complained often to Father about the losses incurred to her income because of the dire situation; and I both feared and hoped that these losses might deepen and finally render her incapable of caring for our family.

But where could we go if we could not stay with her?

Perhaps she and Grandma Digna could share us, I thought. Grandmother Thins could keep Maria and Elisabeth with her. Johannes, too, for while he was difficult, she adored him, perhaps believing that willfulness in a boy child was the sign of an ambitious spirit. Cornelia, Aleydis, Beatrix, and I could go to Grandma Digna, who did not care how proper or pretty we were, who simply loved us.

But our mother would choose to stay with her own mother, I knew—and wherever Mother was, Father must be. Of this, I was certain—so my thoughts stopped there. It was not possible for me to imagine living without my father. In any case, I reminded myself that we could not live with Grandma Digna because she was not Catholic. The warmth and comfort of her household here on earth would be a poor substitute for the eternal comfort of heaven. I tried not to worry about the fact that, for the same reason we could not live with her now, at Mechelen, she would not be in heaven with us when it came time to go.

I prayed to understand why this must be. I prayed that God might make an exception for our dear grandmother, for I could not bear to think of her suffering the fires of Hell.

When I spoke of this to Father, he said, "God knows who is good." But that was all he would say. Though he attended mass faithfully with Mother and willingly gave help to the Jesuit brothers any time they called upon him, he did not like to talk about the difference between the beliefs of the Catholic church and the church of his boyhood.

Sometimes, though, crossing Great Markt Square to go to the St. Luke's Guild, we heard the organ playing in the Nieuwe Kerk and slipped in to listen. Father's father was buried in a shadowy corner, away from the tradesmen doing business, the women gossiping, the children playing marbles on the smooth tombstones, and we would stand there listening for a while—our only company an occasional friendly dog that had wandered in off the square.

The pulpit was always empty at these times. The predicant allowed the organ to be played only before and after their services and sometimes at midday, in hopes of drawing people away from the taverns. It would have been a sin for Father and me, as Catholics, to enter the reformed church during their worship, so I could only imagine the predicant's harsh voice echoing in this sanctuary built for song. I could only imagine, too, how the church had looked before the Protestants smashed the stained glass windows and stripped it of its saints and treasures.

Still, it was so beautiful inside. On cloudy days, the light falling through the vast, clear windows dimmed and brightened, flickered and receded—rather like music, it seemed to me. This observation had made Father smile. He told me that he had said exactly the same thing to his own father many years ago.

He brushed a finger along the line of my jaw, as if drawing it. "How your grandfather would have delighted in you, Carelina," he said.

And while I felt joy at his words, I felt grief, too—for the different life we might have had with our dear grandfather in it.

Perhaps due to her financial difficulties, Grandmother became increasingly obsessed with Uncle Willem's affairs. Once he had been committed to Heer Taerling's house of correction, she pored over her account books, making careful notations of every expense she undertook for his care and in the settling of his many debts. Then she petitioned to gain custody of his properties so that she might claim the rents to offset what she had spent. But just when her petition had been approved and she was satisfied that, at last, Uncle Willem's life was under her control, he fell in love.

Mary Gerrits was the object of his affection. She was a housemaid in Heer Taerling's house, which would have been enough to make Grandmother determine to put a stop to the affair right from the start, if only she had had knowledge of it. As it was, she was not aware of anything amiss until Heer Taerling appeared at her house one Sunday evening, hat in hand, to tell her that Uncle Willem had likely run away.

He had by then earned occasional in-and-out privileges, and Heer Taerling told Grandmother that his wife, Maeyken, had last seen Willem in the company of Mary Gerrits that morning, the two of them setting off for church. Later in the day, Mary came back to the house alone. When questioned about Willem's absence, she swore she knew nothing about it. When Heer Taerling searched Willem's room and found his trunk and most of his clothing missing, she swore she knew nothing about that either.

She was but a poor servant girl from Bommel, she wailed. She had come to Delft seeking employment, for she could not longer bear to stay in the house of her stepfather and see her poor mother abused. She wanted only to take care of herself and to live an honest life. It was not fair to implicate her in something she did not even understand.

But soon after Heer Taerling's visit, Mary disappeared from Heer Taerling's house herself. Then, in a matter of weeks, we learned that Mary and Willem were betrothed. I had never seen Grandmother so agitated. Her wrath at this turn of events was such that even Maria and little Johannes, her favorites, avoided her for fear of finding themselves caught in its swath. Mother wept constantly. Cornelia and I occupied ourselves at our household tasks and cared for the little ones, keeping them as quiet as we could.

Father painted through the tempest, lost in his beautiful musical interiors. When I had finished the work I must do for him each morning, I pulled one of the lion's head chairs that he was not using to a shadowy place near his easel and sat, spellbound, watching his hand. It moved like a musician's hand, each small gesture making its own precise note.

Each time Father made one of these paintings, I was certain it was the most beautiful painting in the world. Perhaps *The Music Lesson*, the last of these musical paintings, truly was. I knew that I should never, ever forget the black and gold virginal with its graceful, rhythmic frieze of sea horses; the yellow light falling in through the elegantly leaded window, illuminating the top of the instrument upon which Father had painted MUSICA LETITIAE COMES MEDICINA DOLORUM—*Music is the companion of joy, the balm of sorrow.*

There were but two figures in the painting: a woman standing

109

at the virginal, her back to the viewer, and a man watching her, his hand resting on a cane. As if to separate them from the rest of the world, Father had painted a large table in the right foreground, with a Turkish carpet and a white porcelain jug upon it that were so lovely the eye could not help but stop and examine them. Behind the table was one of the blue lion's head chairs set so that anyone claiming it would find himself facing away from the couple. The bold geometric design of the black and white floor demanded its own attention.

Cleverly, though, Father made the vanishing point just to the left of the woman's sleeve. This served to agitate the viewer, making his eyes want to make their way slowly through the complicated fore-ground at the same time they wanted to travel directly to the lovers.

They were lovers, I know that now. The painting is drenched in love. The warm sun falling in through the window, the aching richness of color. And the woman's face like a secret in the mirror above the instrument: only in the reflection, can the viewer see her shy glance toward the man.

Part of Father's easel is reflected in the mirror, too. A cause of further agitation, for even as the viewer intrudes upon this private moment between the lovers, the easel tells its own secret. This is a painted moment, not real.

Father was putting the finishing touches on the painting, when Grandmother appeared in the doorway and insisted that he must instantly turn his attention to finding Uncle Willem. Heer Taerling's wife, Maeyken, was with her—a busy, thin, bird-like woman—and Grandmother bade her tell Father all she knew.

Mary had lied to them from the beginning, Maeyken said in a trembling voice. She had claimed a suitor in Bommel and begged permission to go there and speak with her parents about his proposal of marriage. They did not consent to it, she said when she returned. Instead, she had been betrothed to a cattleman from Waelwijck and meant to learn the trade of selling silk in a shop so that she could work as a shopkeeper after her marriage.

In fact, there had been no suitors at all; Mary had no family in Bommel. She was from The Hague, where she was known as a thief. It must be so, Maeyken said—for Mary had taken laundry from her house, and a purse with a silver handle was missing. Mary had watched Maeyken hide the purse in the straw beneath her bed. Only she could have taken it.

Even worse, Maeyken said, her other housemaid, Maertge, confessed that Mary had asked her many questions about Willem and, upon learning of his considerable assets, had confided her intention to marry him. Mary told Maertge that she knew Uncle Willem's rich mother would never agree to the union, so she planned to pretend that Uncle Willem had made her pregnant. Laughing, she had bound herself up with a cushion on her belly and laced her bosom loosely to show Maertge how she planned to trick Grandmother into believing this was so. Also, Maergtge told Maeyken, she had overheard Mary tell Uncle Willem that Heer Taerling meant to suspend his in-and-out privileges and confine him to the house again. That was how she had convinced him to run away. Indeed, she had sent word to Maergtge, crowing news of their betrothal.

Maeyken's words hung in the air, resonant as chords struck on an organ.

"Johannes, you must find him," Grandmother said. "He is likely in Gouda. It is what he knows. You must go today."

It was in his own interest and the interest of his children to do so, she told him. For if Uncle Willem were actually to have a child with this horrid, scheming woman, half of Grandmother's assets must go to it upon her death.

Father sighed and set down his paintbrush.

I begged Father to let me go with him, but he said I must stay and help Mother, who was with child once again. She had been frightened since Uncle Willem's disappearance. Often, I heard her wake in the night and cry out his name, just as she had on the day he had tried to beat her with his stick. Indeed, she dreamed of that terrible day again and again. I knew this, for I had heard her tell Father. I had heard his low voice reassuring her that Uncle Willem was nowhere near. But she could not be comforted.

Mother wept when she learned that Father must go in search of him. She feared Father might come to harm by Uncle Willem's hand. She feared, too, that Uncle Willem might learn that Father was absent from our household and sneak back into Delft to bedevil her. The moment the door closed behind him, she took to her bed and drew the curtains.

Grandmother excused Cornelia from her chores to play the virginal in the hope that music might rouse our mother and set her emotions right, but Mother made her stop. She did not want to hear anything beautiful. Until she heard our father's voice again, until she knew that she was safe from Uncle Willem, she did not want to hear anything at all. She did not even want to hear our prayers.

This made Grandmother press her lips together so tightly that the skin around them went white, and it occurred to me—not without some pleasure—that our mother was defying her. Grandmother stomped around the house, her keys rattling at her waist. Mother lay silent upon her pillows. Before the afternoon had passed, Grandmother had decided to ignore her. If she could not assert her will upon her son or daughter, there was always poor Tanneke, who could be depended upon to quake in her presence.

Ours was the cleanest house in Papists' Corner, perhaps in all of

Delft, but that did not keep Grandmother from bidding her to strip each room of its furniture and then scrub and scour the floors with sand. We children were put to work as well. Maria and Elisabeth polished the tables and cabinets, the brass and silver until they shone. Cornelia and I washed the walls and windows, helped by Aleydis and Beatrix who had been instructed to clean as high as they could reach with a damp cloth. Even Johannes was given a task. He must drape the cloth Grandmother gave him over one finger and rub it in the nooks and crannies where Tanneke's larger fingers could not reach.

If this upheaval further distressed our mother, she did not speak of it. She kept to her bed, the curtains drawn, and we worked around her. If she cried in the night, I did not know it; for I was exhausted from my labors and slept like the dead. Even my mind's eye was blank. If I had been able to steal moments in Father's painting room, even if he had replenished my supplies, I doubt I could have summoned the will to pick up the brush and begin.

Three days passed, and then four. When Father returned on the fifth day, a contrite, bedraggled Uncle Willem in tow, I burst into tears. Tanneke drew me close to her and held me tight, believing that I was afraid of Uncle Willem. She would not permit Willem to come near me, she whispered. Any moment, Mijnheer Taerling would come to take him away. But it was the sight of Father that had made me cry. It was not until he returned safely that I realized how frightened I had been. What if he had come to some harm? What if we had been left without him forever?

It was a sad story that he told us once Heer Taerling had come and taken Uncle Willem away. When Mary Gerrits followed our uncle to Gouda, she asked him to marry her, and he said yes. He told her where to find his father's mourning mantle and instructed her to take it and pawn it so that they would have money to travel to Waelwijck to tell her family the good news. But when they got there, he began to realize that much of what she had told him of her life had been a lie. He remembered how, when he sent her to pawn the mantle, she had kept back some of the money and bought herself some new stockings and a little gold ring. Still, he loved her and allowed the marriage bans to be issued, despite the knowledge that she would surely deceive him again. He admitted to Father that he would indeed have gone through with the marriage had Grandmother not objected so vehemently to his intentions that word of it had traveled all the way to Gouda and frightened him into sending Mary away.

It was long past morning when all was told and both Mother and Grandmother were satisfied that Uncle Willem would no longer be a threat to any of us. Nonetheless, Father climbed the stairs to his painting room when he was through. He looked at the painting of the man and woman at the virginal, still on the easel. Then, though I was there to do his bidding, he went to the grinding slab and prepared his own palette, in yellows and browns. In broad strokes, he made the shape of a tenor viol, as if abandoned at the woman's feet. He must cover part of her red skirt and several squares of the marble floor to put it there: one more barrier between the viewer and the lovers. As if adding the tenor viol could keep the world away.

The affair with Mary Gerrits had finally frightened Uncle Willem into submission; and henceforth, he not only remained docilely in Heer Taerling's care, but gave over his power of attorney to Grandmother so that she could manage his assets and oversee his lands near Schoonhaven. She was, by this time, in her seventy-third year, and did not wish to risk her health traveling to collect rents and make certain that Uncle Willem's tenants maintained his properties to her high standards. So Father must take time from his work and do it for her. He knew nothing of such matters at the outset, but was conscientious by nature; and, in time, he acquitted himself so well that Grandmother began to send him to Gouda and sometimes Amsterdam to tend to her own properties in these cities.

He did not complain. When I asked him once whether he thought it unfair that Grandmother did not give him some share of the profits from the properties he oversaw, he reminded me of how many years she had cared for us at considerable expense.

"But if she paid you for your work, perhaps she would not need to care for us any longer," I said. "We could have a house of our own."

"Your mother—" He shook his head. "It is difficult for her; she is not strong. I'm not at all sure she would be up to managing a household herself, even if we were able to afford it. No, *dochterken*. We are better off here, with Mother Thins. She is a bigger help to us than you know."

He was right, of course. Even if it had been possible to move, it would put too great a burden on our mother to do so. In truth, I had been resigned to living with Grandmother Thins long ago; and during the time Father had made me his helper, I had not been wholly discontent in her house. But now his travels kept him away from home so much that he had little time to paint and, of course, no time at all to resume my lessons.

Had I been a boy, Grandmother might have apprenticed me to a master painter to continue my education. Father had many friends in Amsterdam—and, of course, Heer Hoogstraaten in Dordrecht, who would have been glad to take me. Father had schooled me well in the basics of the craft and I could have been trained quickly to be of help to them. But Grandmother would not hear of it. A girl could not leave her home and live among young men in a painter's workshop.

Nor could I work alone in Father's painting room when he was gone. His daily routine, which had claimed me in the mornings, held no precedent in his absence. I must work with Tanneke in the kitchen or help Cornelia care for the little ones all through the day. In the evening, though , when they were finally put to bed, I would go and sit among Father's paints and easels. I did not waste a candle, but let the moonlight fall in on me. Washed in it, my hands seemed painted in lead-white, and I posed them this way and that, imagining them fixed in paint, framed in silence. I could not keep them still for long; but must flex my fingers, aching as they were to hold a brush.

It overtook me like a fever, this desire to paint everything I saw. Rain on the cobblestones, clouds scudding across the sky. I wanted to paint Tanneke's strong forearms, Aleydis's springy yellow hair, Mother's sad, beautiful eyes. The cat skulking in the alley behind the Jesuit's house, I longed to paint with quick, bold strokes of cream and ginger. Even Grandmother Thins's stern face compelled me.

So great was my need to feel the rhythm of the brush that my nerves were frayed by it. I was given to outbursts of anger, wont to burst into tears for no good reason. Thinking it was womanhood come upon me, Tanneke sat me down in the kitchen and explained what I already knew. But I did not begin my monthly bleeding, as Maria had done. Nor did my body begin to take on a new shape.

It was willfulness, in Grandmother's view. Father had spoiled me with his impractical idea of teaching me to paint. I must grow accustomed to doing my household duties now that I was no longer a child. But it was not willfulness. I had no will. Indeed, it seemed to me at times that there were no bones in my body. I would gaze out the window, thinking how I must have long streaming hairs in my brush to paint the grasses floating on the surface of the canal. I would stare endlessly at the white line the sun drew, defining the Nieuwe Kerk's bell tower against the sky.

Only Father might have understood my sudden change in temperament, but the strain of his new responsibilities had taken its toll on his own good humor and on his concentration. When he returned home after one of his trips, he must attend to Mother, who had missed him sorely and must tell him of every ache and indignity she had suffered in his absence. He must hear Grandmother's complaints about us children and take us aside, one by one, and try to ease our various discontents. Once in his painting room, he would often sit on his three-cornered stool, brush in hand, and stare at whatever he had left unfinished, as if trying to remember why he had begun it and what he had hoped it might be.

A year passed, then another. Father painted but occasionally: paintings so small that he could nearly frame them, laying his thumbs and first fingers against the canvas in a square. A girl wearing a red hat, a girl holding a flute, a girl making lace. Were they faces he had seen on the canal boat, fellow passengers? Or in a tavern, where he had taken a meal? In the market square of some city? I did not ask, just helped him as best I could and hoped, soon, he would come back to us.

# THE ART
## OF PAINTING

HE GUILD House was on the Voldersgracht, the most beautiful street in our town. On one side of the street were fine brick houses; on the other, the canal, which like a long canvas, held in it a rippling reflection of the backs of the buildings that lined Great Markt Square, complete with flowers cascading from wooden window boxes and the delicate pattern of lace curtains. Indeed, had Father wanted to paint one of the streets inside his imagined *View of Delft*, it might have looked exactly like this street that God had painted on the water.

Entering the house with Father, I always felt so proud. His fellow guildsmen greeted him with both affection and respect. They smiled and winked at me, and I was invited to sit at the big table in the dining hall, where the board of headmen gathered to consider their affairs—even given a drop of wine in one of their fine crested goblets. It was a grand room, with a carved oak fireplace, velvet curtains drawn back from leaded windows, and a proud display of every kind of work done by the guild members. Paintings, sculptures, glassware, embroidered tapestries. Platters, vases, and candlesticks made of the fine blue and white porcelain named for our town.

While the men talked, I gazed about me, almost always settling upon the self-portrait of Mijnheer Fabritius that hung above the sideboard: the plain, eternally young face of the man who had been my father's dearest friend. I wondered what he might have painted had he lived, how, over the years, his companionship might have eased Father's many burdens. And I wished, as I had wished for as long as I could remember, that I might have known him.

When the meeting at the Guild House was through, the guildsmen retired to Mechelen for their customary glass of ale. There, all talk was of the Harmony. The war with England was virtually won, and "The Perpetual Edict for the Preserving of Freedom" was laid before the States of Holland, an embodiment of Mijnheer De Witt's vision of harmony for our land. It would abolish the stadtholderate forever and transfer power to each provincial state, and was seen by writers, poets, and artists as the supreme embodiment of the True Freedom.

For Delft, with its many Catholic citizens, the Perpetual Edict was good news, as well, for it was bound to undermine Church authority, thus broadening toleration for our beliefs. Indeed, the mood in Papists' Corner was lighter than it had been for some time. Even Grandmother seemed hopeful, though I suspect it was less the prospect of harmony among men that set her humming about her household tasks than the improvement of her personal finances that had occurred with the ending of the hostilities.

Her happier financial state meant just one thing to me: Father was home more than he had been in a long while. We needed him, for we were all still deeply saddened by the loss of our infant brother, Antony. And shocked, too, for he had been taken from us suddenly, for no reason that we knew. His last day on earth had been a day like any other; and at the end of it, Mother had put him in his cradle, healthy and well-fed. She had slept soundly herself, and was surprised and pleased to wake past daylight, for she thought that, finally, Antony had slept through the night. But when she reached into the cradle, she found his little body cold as ice. Her cries had brought us all running to the front room, where we found her collapsed on the floor, holding Antony close to her—as if the warmth of her body might revive him.

Had the devil taken him? Tanneke feared that he had, for he was known to roam about in moonlight and snatch the souls of children while they slept.

Father Jans said no. He had baptized Antony himself and was certain the child was now an angel in heaven with our Lord. But this had not kept our mother from falling ill with grief.

Nor the fact that there were so many of us children now, Grandmother's house was full to bursting. After Johannes: Gertruyd, Franciscus, and Catharina. And yet another on the way.

So it was good that Father was near. He alone could make her smile; and his presence calmed the little ones, too—especially Johannes, who remained a difficult, cantankerous child. Best, he had reclaimed my mornings. I woke with a feeling of anticipation for the day ahead and crept from my sleeping cupboard, anxious to discover what task I would be given. Even the most ordinary work delighted me. Anything I did in the painting room was more enjoyable than housework and caring for the children.

He took me with him to Mechelen, too. In the past year or so, Grandma Digna's health had declined; and now that Father was again spending most of his time in Delft, he felt compelled to help her with the business of the tavern when he could. If Grandmother Thins was unhappy about the time he spent there, she did not speak of it: Grandma Digna was his mother, after all, and must be honored for that reason. She did not even grumble much about my going along to help. I was busy every moment I was there, Father assured her.

This was true. While Father and Grandma went over the account books, I helped Jutte with the cleaning. Inside, we polished the brass, washed the furniture, scoured the floors with sand; outside, we used a device that sprayed water as high as the roof to clean the building itself. Sometimes I helped Jutte serve the customers, as well. In and out of the kitchen I went, catching snippets of talk between Father and Grandma. She basked in his presence, bade him tell her about his work. Something different from anything he had ever done was gathering in his mind's eye, I heard him say.

Thus, I was not surprised when I entered the painting room one morning to see him preparing a canvas near the size his *View of Delft* had been. He asked me to sort through his store of oils and pigments to ascertain what was at hand, so that we might go to Mijnheer de Cocq to buy supplies.

"Jan Vermeer!" the apothecary called out when we entered his shop. "You are painting again? You have another commission from van Ruijven?"

"I am soon to be painting," Father said. "Yes. But it is not a commissioned work; so I must beg your indulgence, for I cannot yet pay you fully for all I need."

Mijnheer deCocq simply nodded. He wrote as Father listed these needs, then made a bill for what would be owed him. Father signed it. I wondered if Grandmother knew of his intention to make an uncommissioned painting; but I did not worry unduly, for I knew that Mijnheer van Ruijven was always willing to purchase any painting Father made.

Indeed, he had purchased Father's last work—a painting of my sister Maria, which had been completed in the spring. He had dressed her in a loose antique robe and a blue turban with a sash, which he painted swinging forward. Her collar was a thick slash of white that balanced the tilt of her jaw. She wore Mother's pearl earring, and the pattern of light Father painted upon it made it seem globe-like, its own little world. The Maria that emerged from his brush was one I had never seen before: wistful, her head turned as if to take one last glance at her childhood.

Tears filled Mother's eyes when she saw the painting. Even Grandmother declared it a wonder, though she did not understand why Father had hidden Maria's pretty golden hair under the turban, or why he had not portrayed her at some domestic task, so that the viewer might see her virtue as well as her charm. And, though she could not be sorry that Mijnheer van Ruijven decided to purchase the work, she did not at all approve of a painting of her granddaughter hanging in his house for anyone to see. If Mijnheer van Ruijven wanted a picture of a young lady, she said, why not commission Father to paint a portrait of his Magdalena.

"Mijnheer van Ruijven knows I do not paint portraits," Father said.

"Ach, Johannes." Grandmother sighed in frustration. "What is this then, if not a portrait of Maria?"

Matter-of-factly, he answered, "A girl with a pearl earring."

The words eased something inside me. Maria was a girl with a pearl earring to our father, no more. I was his helper; perhaps, someday, a painter in my own right. And the painting was done. I no longer needed to suffer the daily indignities of my sister's conceit. But for our continuing dependence on Grandmother Thins's resources and Mother's enduring sadness, I was happy during that summer of the Harmony.

Father was happy, too. The canvas prepared for the new painting, the supplies bought, he set to gathering objects in his sun-lit corner. Then, one by one, he took up each object and held it before the light, learning it as a child would learn a lesson. I watched, curious, for these were not the same objects he had painted in the past. A book, a mask, a trumpet. A hanging tapestry, red-fringed chairs, a brass chandelier, a black velvet hat. Green satin, a thin volume of music, a laurel crown. A map of our land. Each object deepened the mystery of what world his new painting would reveal.

Then he bade me call Maria.

The shock of his request stays with me still—and the hurt I felt; for I knew instantly that he meant to make her the center of this work. I wanted to leave the painting room, walk down the stairs, and out of Grandmother's house forever. Of course, I did not. Nor could I be angry at my father, for I knew he had not meant to hurt me. I did what he asked. And when Maria came to stand before him, he placed the laurel crown upon her head.

She is an object to him, I told myself. No more. An object in a constellation of objects, her face no more compelling to him than the fold or shine of the blue robe he has dressed her in, or the way the blue-green leaves of the laurel crown lay against her yellow hair. But I could not believe it.

Only Cornelia understood. And wordlessly, in her way. A light touch on my shoulder when she caught me brooding. Some chore done. Flowers she picked for me while the little ones were at play. I was grateful for her sympathy and for the nature of its expression. I was ashamed of what I felt, and did not want to speak of it. I could not have spoken without crying, in any case—and what would have been the good in that? I could only go about the tasks that Father gave me with the knowledge that there would always be a place for me in his painting room; whereas, when he had finished the painting of Maria, she would be sent back to her ordinary life. Of this life, I was in no way envious. It was her life on the canvas that pained me— eternal life. A blasphemous thought, I knew—as if to live in Father's painting were the same as to live in heaven with our Lord. I prayed to be forgiven for it.

I took some comfort knowing that Maria was blind to the painting's true meaning. She was the center of it—that was all she knew;

when, in fact, it was not about her at all. But the small pleasure of this intelligence was greatly outweighed by what else I understood as weeks and then months passed, and *The Art of Painting* emerged beneath Father's brush. In it was every single thing he knew. Long after his real life had been forgotten, Maria would remain—to any worthy eye, the consummate teacher of all he had been.

Nights, I woke in a fever of envy and watched her sleep. In the moonlight that fell through the bed curtains, her face looked pale as an angel's: the same face Father painted by day, eyelids lowered, as if sleeping where she stood. It was worse not to look at her; for if I closed my eyes I saw the painting before me. Maria, the muse: a trumpet in one hand, a thick yellow volume of Thucydides folded to her heart. Father dressed in an elegant split doublet, a black velvet hat perched jauntily on his head. He was seated at his easel, his back to the viewer, his brush raised to the blue leaves of the laurel wreath he was painting near the top of the canvas within the canvas. Behind them, Visscher's map: "Seventeen Provinces of the Netherlands," proclaiming NOVA DESCRIPTIO. As if they two, alone, described the world it portrayed.

Days were no better, for Maria treated me as she did when I must help her prepare for parties in the evenings.

"Carelina, I am thirsty," she would say, and bid me fetch her a cup of water.

Or, "Carelina, I am so warm in these heavy garments. Could you wipe my brow?"

I despised myself, serving her this way. Worse, I longed to *be* her, beautiful in Father's eyes, worthy of his brush—and this disturbed me more than anything; for, in the past, I had never wanted to be anyone but myself. I had grown accustomed to my plain face, or so I thought. It was like my father's face; and, in this, I had found satisfaction. But now I could not bear the sight of it.

Dear Tanneke. She seemed to know when I could not bear the confines of Grandmother's household another moment, and sent me off on invented errands so that I might have some time alone. I would wander the streets of our town, stopping at a market stand to stare at the glitter of fish scales, or on a bridge to toss a pebble and shatter the glassy reflection of trees and houses painted on the canal. Such distraction made me clumsy; and in my wanderings, I often stumbled or stepped into the path of townspeople passing by.

But the world works in strange and wonderful ways; and so it was that I was walking one day, contemplating the geometry of gables against the sky, and my distraction propelled me so directly and startlingly into a lady that I lost my balance and fell backwards.

"Why, you are Vermeer's daughter!" she said, helping me up from where I had sprawled on the street. The fruit that had been in her market basket when we collided rolled off, ruined, into the gutter, but she did not seem to notice it. "Carelina, is it?"

I nodded, yes. I tried to apologize for the trouble I had caused her; but she hushed me with the wave of her hand and said, "I am Maria van Oosterwijck. Your father and I, we were students together many years ago."

Now, thinking of this moment, I see the path that opened up to me and I am flooded with gratitude for all that I have known traveling upon it, all that I am yet to know and see. Then I was only all the more embarrassed for the knowledge that I had very nearly harmed a woman who was not only my father's friend, but an acclaimed painter as well. I stood gaping, speechless before her. But she went on as if our chance encounter had brought nothing but pleasure.

"Indeed, your father has told me about you—what a help you are to him. I see him in the square now and then, you know." She raised her hand toward the handsome brick house behind us. "I live here," she said. "Will you come in and let my Geertje fix you a drink?

Tea perhaps. And a nice cake. To calm you after such a nasty fall." Her eyes brown eyes twinkled. "I should give you some fruit as well, if you had not sent it all flying into the street."

I blushed. Her teasing words did not hurt my feelings, though; indeed, they made my heart lighten; and I smiled for the first time in a long while. "Yes, please," I said. "I would like that." And followed her inside.

She led me through a front hall to the place where she worked. It was a big room, lined with windows. It smelled of oils and pigments, as Father's painting room did; but there was the scent of flowers, too. On that day, a bouquet of ordinary garden flowers in a blue and white Chinese vase, exotic in their abundance. There were painted flowers, too. A half-finished painting on an easel; a dozen or so finished, framed paintings hung on the walls. In one corner of the room was a little table with chairs drawn up to it, and Mejuffrouw van Oosterwijck bade me sit down.

"Geertje!" she called. "Geertje!"

A woman appeared, smiling. She was near Mejuffrow van Oosterwijck's age, perhaps a few years older, and they might have been sisters for the familiar way they greeted one another. They did not look at all like sisters, though. Mejuffrouw van Oosterwijck was small and lithe, with a heart-shaped face and brown hair curling out from beneath her cap. Geertje was sturdy and blond. She must be Mejuffrouw van Oosterwijck's maid, I thought, for Mejuffrouw van Oosterwijck directed her to prepare tea and cakes; but when she brought the tray into Mejuffrouw van Oosterwijck' painting room, there were three cups and plates on it, and she sat down at the table with us.

While Geertje poured the tea, Mejuffrouw explained. "Geertje has been with me since we were girls," she said. "We have been dear friends ever since—and fellow painters for many years, as well.

Geertje is a great help to me in every way. I could not do without her."

Geertje smiled and set a cup of green tea at before me.

Green tea! I had thought I must wait until I was grown to taste it. Now I took my first sip, breathed in the exotic scent of it, and felt as if the world had entered me. I heard Grandmother's voice at the edges of my consciousness, reproving me for such an indulgence, but I did not listen to it. I drank the tea down and allowed Geertje to pour me another cup, all the while listening to Mejuffrouw van Oosterwijck talk about painting.

Her voice was melodious, like no other voice I had ever heard. The sound of her laughter was like little bells. "It was as if I had been born to it," she said. "When I was a child at school, I was constantly caught drawing on my slate instead of tending to my lessons. Flowers, always flowers. Father indulged me in the beginning; drawing flowers seemed a suitable activity for a little girl. So . . . pretty." She laughed. "What age are you, Carelina?"

"Nearly fourteen," I said, "in October."

She nodded, took a sip of her tea. "So I thought. It was at the same age that I told my Father I wanted to learn to paint." She turned to Geertje. "Was he not scandalized?"

"Oh, yes," Geertje said.

Mejuffrouw van Oosterwijck smiled. "And I did not even tell him then that I meant to *be* a painter!" she went on. "Nor that I meant to teach Geertje all I learned so that we might spend our lives painting together. God rest his soul. It was quite enough for him to consider allowing me to learn the craft at all, let alone consider that I intended to devote my whole life to it.

"Mijnheer van Aelst taught me first," she went on. "He was a painter of flowers himself, as you no doubt know. Later, I convinced Father to send me to Antwerp, so that I might study with the great master of flower painting, Mijnheer de Heem. But I was not quite so independent as I had thought myself to be, for I missed Father and Geertje terribly." She gestured to include the cozy room. "And my home here, as well. So I returned to Delft in a year's time, and here I have been since. And shall no doubt stay for the rest of my life. Like your own father, Carelina. So many are gone now; but he remained to earn his keep here, as I did."

Mejuffrouw van Oosterwijck earned much more than her keep. Kings and emperors were among her patrons, and paid dearly for her work. Indeed, Emperor Leopold I of Austria had been so pleased by his commissioned piece that he sent her portraits of himself and the empress in diamond-studded frames. I knew this, for Father had told me.

"I am glad for his presence here in Delft," she said. "I greatly admire his work and have never forgotten the time that we were students together with Mijnheer van Aelst. He was kind to me, and respectful of my intentions to become a painter when others made me feel that, being a girl, I was not wanted. We two were so . . . *fervent* about our lessons. We would leave Mijnheer van Aelst's studio and walk along the street together, talking about everything under the sun. Even now, we have much to say to each other when we meet by chance. And I am able to see his work, for Mijnheer van Ruijven was a dear friend of my father and I am often invited to dine with his family. Your father is at work on something new, I have heard. Something as large as his *View of Delft*. And equally astounding."

"Yes," I said. Then, to my dismay, I started to cry. A sudden, quiet release of tears, as if a dyke had broken inside me. They ran steadily down my face, and I sat, helpless, my hands in my lap.

Mejuffrouw van Oosterwijck did not ask me to explain, just put her hand on mine. Geertje poured another cup of tea, set the last little cake upon my plate to comfort me; and for the first time in my life, I felt as if I were the center of the universe. Their universe of paint and cakes and tea and flowers.

Later, back at Grandmother's house, the memory of their kindness to me was like a dream. If I closed my eyes, I could see Mejuffrouw van Oosterwijck's painting room and the blur of her garden beyond the windows. I must come again tomorrow, she said when I left. We would have tea and cakes again, like three ladies. And, if I wished, she would show me how she went about the work of making her paintings of flowers.

I would like that very much, I told her. Blushing, for as I spoke I heard Mijnheer van Hoogstraaten's voice in my head: "Painters of flowers? They are but common soldiers in the army of art!" He would be coming soon, I knew, for Father was putting the finishing touches on *The Art of Painting*, and he would want to see it. Would he disapprove of my new friendship?

Father would not disapprove. Of this, I was certain. Indeed, he always spoke with admiration of Mejuffrouw van Oosterwijk, and would be pleased to know that I had made her acquaintance. Yet when I returned home that afternoon, I did not tell him of our meeting. Nor did I tell Cornelia. Nor Tanneke, though her eyes told me she knew something had happened.

I could barely sleep that night; and the next morning in Father's painting studio, I was so distracted by the promise of returning to Mejuffrouw van Oosterwijck's house that, for the first time, I could look at the image of Maria on the canvas and see what Father saw: Clio, muse of history, a face crafted of shadow and light. Our midday meal seemed endless, bearable only for the knowledge that once it was finally through, I would hurry through Tanneke's errands and visit Mejuffouw van Oosterwijck and Geertje again.

But when I reached the house, I was struck with shyness. When, finally, I gathered the courage to knock, the sound was so faint, even to my own ears, that I was certain no one would hear it. But soon I heard footsteps. The door opened, and Geertje's face lit up in a smile.

"Maria! Carelina has come," she called.

Mejuffrouw van Oosterwijck hurried from the back of the house. She greeted me, taking my hands in hers, squeezing them affectionately. There were flecks of paint in the creases of her knuckles and beneath her fingernails, I noticed. My own hands often looked this way when I was helping Father. A disgrace, Grandmother Thins believed. But if kind Mejuffrouw van Oosterwijck was not ashamed of little paint on her hands, how could it be disgraceful?

In the painting room, we had tea and cakes again, and Mejuffrouw van Oossterwijck asked me about my own work. *My work*, I thought—as if I were a colleague! Perhaps it was the shock of being addressed as her equal that caused me to tell her the truth. I had copied Mijnheer Fabritius's goldfinch under Father's direction a number of times. But his lengthy absences over the past several years had left him no time to continue teaching me. So, mostly, I painted in my head.

I flushed, saying this last thing, for it sounded strange. But Mejuffrouw van Oosterwijck smiled and leaned toward me.

"What do you paint in your head, Carelina?" she asked. "What do you see?"

"Real things," I said. "I mean things in the world. Like the canal grasses: the way they . . ." I paused and wiggled my fingers, for I could not think of a word to describe the way the grasses moved in the water. "Sometimes parts of things. An arm, or a fold of cloth. Perhaps the shell of a beetle. And I paint Fabritius's goldfinch in my head, as well. Having actually painted it, I can remember the feel of the brush

on canvas. And Father keeps it in his painting room, you know—
so it is there for me to see, anytime I wish to remember it exactly. He
says that in *The Goldfinch* there is everything a painter needs to
know . . ."

I could not continue, embarrassed by the earnestness of my own
voice.

"You are named for him, are you not?" Mejuffrouw van Oosterwijck said thoughtfully. "Fabritius. I believe I remember your father
telling me that."

"Yes," I said. "I was born on the day of his death."

"The day of the powder blast?" Geertje asked.

I nodded.

Mejuffrouw van Oosterwijck shuddered. "I shall never forget
that! The sound, oh! And then to hear Fabritius was lost in it. What
a blessing that he had left the goldfinch in your father's keeping. It
is a wondrous little thing. Indeed, there is no better teacher than a
perfect work of art." She gestured me toward the corner where her
easel stood. Hanging near it, easily in her view if she glanced up from
her canvas, was a framed watercolor tulip. "There is *my* goldfinch,"
she said. "Judith Leyster's tulip. *My* idea of perfection."

It was not large: a single tulip done in watercolor. Its petals, just
beginning to open, were pearl white, streaked with crimson. Long,
elegant leaves curved up from the bottom of the stem. I looked hard
at it, thinking of Mijnheer Fabritius's goldfinch and how, upon close
examination, the bird dissolved into a blur of colors; but no matter
how hard I looked at the tulip floating on the rich vellum, it remained
a tulip. This shocked me, for I was accustomed to Father's way of
rendering the world: his fascination with light and shadow, the
subtlety with which he altered perspective. I expected the world of
the painting to dissolve if I got too close to it, the way the goldfinch

did. Now here was this tulip, pickable, real. Yet it held my eye as Father's paintings did.

I did not know how to think of it, or what to say. Thankfully, Mejuffrouw van Oosterwijck did not seem to expect a response. She went to a big oak linen cupboard and opened the door. I saw no linens in it, though. Instead, the shelves were lined with many small boxes, each with a different kind of flower painted on the front. There were vases and jars, painting supplies.

Mejuffrouw van Oosterwijck set a dozen or so of the boxes on a long table, and I saw that each was filled with paper flowers that had been cut out and painted in various sizes, tints, and stages of bloom. "Come," she said. "We shall compose a little painting, you and I."

I went to stand beside her at the table.

"Choose," she said. "Anything you like. We are painting, so you may mix the blooms in any way you desire. Season is of no consequence. Nor time. *That* is what I love most about what I do."

And I smiled, for I understood that this was Mejuffrouw van Oosterwijck's way of making a world all her own, as Father made his own world of light.

Yellow roses and tulips, poppies—one in bloom, one showing only a slice of orange in its round, opening bud; buttercups; one purple iris. Geertje took a spray of lilies of the valley from a box and raised an eyebrow, as if to ask my permission to add it. Yes, I nodded. Mejuffrouw van Oosterwijck brought another box from the cupboard; and I laughed when I saw that there were painted insects in it.

It was like child's play, arranging the flowers to create different effects. Mejuffrouw van Oosterwijck and Geertje watched, occasionally reaching over to add to, subtract from, or adjust what I had done.

I was enchanted and bemused by them. In my world, women were stern arbiters of right thoughts and deeds—like Grandmother Thins; or fragile, needy souls—like our mother. There were women like Grandma Digna and Tanneke, of course, who lived to provide sustenance and comfort to those they loved. But I had never known women who were affectionate and playful together, as Mejuffrouw van Oosterwijck and Geertje were. Women who seemed perfectly happy and capable, living in a household where there was no man to take care of them.

In time, I told Father of my acquaintance with Mejuffrouw van Oosterwijck, and it pleased him, as I had known it would. Indeed, when next the two met they spoke of me, and it was decided that— in addition to my morning duties in his painting room—I might visit Mejuffrouw van Oosterwijck two afternoons a week to help her and Geertje with chores in the painting room and in the garden. For this help, Mejuffrouw van Oosterwijck would guide me in exploring the art of flower painting.

I was especially grateful for this time away from Grandmother's house, for Mother was in confinement again. Her stomach had swelled almost obscenely, larger and rounder with this child than any other. By the seventh month, she had grown so awkward and cumbersome that she could barely move, and spent most days lying miserably abed.

Why must she suffer so, I wondered. Why must we all suffer the presence of another infant, who would further disrupt Grandmother's already chaotic household? Each night I knelt on the worn carpet beside my bed and prayed to God that I might understand why He would send Mother and Father another child, when they had so many already and so much hardship caring for them. I prayed, too, that I might learn to love this new brother or sister that was coming.

Cornelia would be the one whose life was most affected by another child, yet she was the one who most looked forward to its arrival. She was happy among the little ones, she told me—not the least bit resentful for my good fortune in escaping to Mejuffrouw van Oosterwijck's house. Indeed, she delighted in it, bidding me tell her about all I experienced there.

I described the wonders of Mejuffrouw's painting cabinet, the little round table in the cozy painting room set prettily for tea. I described the garden, still full of color despite the lateness of the season. Lobelia, phlox. Michaelmas daisies. Sweet peas winding up through the arbor. Flax, autumn crocuses, coreopsis. And sunflowers, which Mejuffrouw van Oosterwijck loved the best. It pleased her to think that God had taken the time to create such an ordinary flower, she said—as if to remind us that every single thing in His universe had been made by His hand to a purpose.

Geertje had teased her that day, I told Cornelia, claiming that her own favorite flower was the Cupid's Dart that Mijnheer van Aelst had planted there.

"Geertje!" Mejuffrouw van Oosterwijck, feigning disapproval. Then laughed, when Geertje told me the story behind the plant. Some years ago, Van Aelst had been quite in love with Mejuffrouw van Oosterwijck and brought it over from his own garden as a gift. Nodding toward the house directly behind theirs, Gertje said, "He lived there then. That window you see through the trees: through it, you could see him working."

"Or *not* working," Mejuffrouw van Oosterwijck said wryly.

Geertje laughed. "Poor man. And your opinion was of such great consequence to him." Turning to me, she went on, "He wanted to marry her, you see. Indeed, he spoke to Mijnheer van Oosterwijck and, with his permission, asked for her hand."

"But I did not want to marry *anyone*," Mejuffrouw van Oosterwijck said. "I was quite busy enough with my work and did not need a husband to attend to as well. Poor Judith Leyster. In all the years she was married to Moelenar, she painted little more than my tulip. He, meanwhile, painted away—with half her talent."

Geertje raised an eyebrow. "Nonetheless, you did not instantly refuse Heer van Aelst."

"Geertje Peters!" Mejuffrouw van Oosterwijck said. "He was lazy as a cat, and you know as well as I do that I as good as refused him when I—*we*—you may remember, as it was your idea to set a requirement we knew he could not possibly fulfill."

A silence fell between them then, and I feared Mejuffrouw van Oosterwijck was a little peeved at her friend. I was greatly relieved when, finally, she burst into merry laughter and said, "Oh, do go on, Geertje. You are bound to tell Carelina all you know, and I might as well be present to hear what you have to say, since it will undoubtedly be necessary to correct you."

"Well," Geertje began. "It *is* true that Maria considered his proposal; indeed, she would have bound to marry him if—"

". . . for one year, every day but Sunday, he spent ten hours a day in his studio," Mejuffrouw van Oosterwick said.

Cornelia laughed when I told her this, delighted as I had been to imagine a man so smitten he would submit to a test at which he was so clearly doomed to fail. Even Father had never worked ten hours every day for a whole year, and I knew no one more dedicated to his work than he was.

"It was cruel." Geertje feigned disapproval. "We could look out the window in the painting room and see if he was working, so we kept a record: a sheet of paper divided into two sections. In one section, we made a mark every time one of us looked out during the prescribed time and saw him at his easel. We made a mark on the other side when he was absent from his place. He was defeated well before the year was up!"

Mejuffrouw van Oosterwijck shrugged her shoulders prettily, her eyes twinkling. "What a happy day it was when, at last, he went off to Amsterdam and left Geertje and me to work in peace," she said. "Though he was a dear man. If I had wanted a husband, I daresay he would have sufficed."

Cornelia marveled at this world on the other side of Delft, never tiring of the stories about Mejuffrouw van Oosterwijck and Geertje. She begged me tell her of Mejuffrouw van Oosterwijck's nephew, Jacobus, as well. The son of her sister, she had raised him from childhood, after the untimely death of his mother. He was a botanist now, recently finished with his studies at the University of Leiden. A solemn young man, tall and thin, with delicate round spectacles perched on his beaky nose, he had returned to Delft to visit his aunt for a time before embarking on his first scientific expedition, to the West Indies.

She listened, rapt, as I recounted his description of the curiosities collected by professors and brought back to the university for study: birds, shells, animals. Herbariums, in which plants were carefully pressed and dried.

"Oh, I should love to hear him speak of these things," Cornelia said. "And, someday, to drink tea with Mejuffrouw van Oosterwijck and Geertje, as well."

I promised her that I should arrange it. Indeed, Cornelia was so enamored of the stories I told her about Mejuffrouw van Oosterwijck's household that when Geertje called to me that she was at the doorstep and must see me, I thought she had got Tanneke to send her with some message so that she might chance a visit. But she was so upset, so clearly frightened that I knew instantly that this was not the case.

It must be the baby coming, I thought—and too early.

"No," Cornelia said. "No, not that."

But when I questioned her further, she could not answer for crying; she gripped my hand, and I hurried along with her in silence, wanting and fearing to know why she had come for me in such a state. Could something have happened to one of the little ones? Or, worse, to our father? I felt as if an iron band had clamped itself around my heart.

But it was Mother who had been hurt. Climbing the stairs to fetch a shawl, she had stepped on a toy that one of the children had left there, and fallen backwards. When Cornelia and I arrived, she was still lying at the bottom of the stairs, white as a sheet, her leg twisted in an unnatural position. She held her arms crossed on her poor swollen belly, as if to cradle the baby inside. Father was bent over her, stroking her hair, whispering some private comfort.

Tanneke had taken Aleydis and the little ones away; Maria and Elisabeth had been sent for Dr. Cuyp; and when they arrived with him, fled upstairs to Grandmother's room, where they lay huddled, useless, weeping. Cornelia sank into a chair in the front room, stunned. Father sat on the step, his head in his hands, while Dr. Cuyp examined Mother. Only Grandmother and I were calm enough to help the doctor move her to her bed.

She cried out only once, when he straightened her leg to splint it. Then she lay, her eyes closed, breathing deeply. She took the rosary Grandmother offered, but her fingers did not move along it. She did not open her eyes when Dr. Cuyp placed his hands on her belly and held them in one place—and then another and another—for moments at a time. When he turned away, he looked troubled. He bade her rest and gestured for Father to follow him to the kitchen.

Tanneke had made a bucket of soapsuds and taken the little ones outside to play in hopes of distracting them. I listened at the window while Father and Dr. Cuyp talked. The boys ran in circles, trailing strings of translucent bubbles in their wake. Gertruy and Beatrix held their scallop shells near their lips and blew big, perfect bubbles, one at a time. Catharina sat on Aleydis's lap and clapped delightedly as they rose and rainbowed in the sun.

"It did not move," Dr. Cuyp told Father.

Fear struck me, for I knew exactly what he meant. A live baby moved inside its mother's womb. Sometimes, when Mother sat quietly, her hands resting on her belly, I saw them rise and then fall again, as the baby turned and settled itself inside her.

"We must wait," Dr. Cuyp said. "And pray. It is all we can do."

In the next days, Grandmother and Tanneke hovered over Mother. Father rarely left her side. I gave up my afternoons with Mejuffrouw van Oosterwijck so that I might help Cornelia and Aleydis keep the little ones from disturbing her. She lay quietly, as she had the day she was hurt, her arms cradling the unborn child. But it did not move, and by the time the birth pains finally began, none of us expected her to bring forth a living child. And so it was. The baby came, silent and blue. Everything perfect about her, but for the fact she did not breathe.

That night, sleepless, I went alone into the back garden. Summer was gone. I shivered in my nightdress; the soles of my feet were cold upon the hard ground. I looked up at the sky, but though the night was clear, I did not see the stars and planets of Mijnheer van Leeuwenhoek's measurable world. I did not see the pictures its constellations made. I saw baby angels, with golden hair and beautiful, delicate wings. Three of them: Gretje, Antony, and the poor, nameless baby I should never have to love.

I returned to Mejuffrouw van Oosterwijck's house only after the baby had been laid to rest. She and Geertje showed me every kindness, bidding me forget about doing chores for them and, instead, lose myself in painting flowers.

They planned an outing into the countryside, as well, and Jacobus accompanied us. We traveled by carriage to the wide sweep of meadow beyond our town, where we sketched grasses and wildflowers, and then collected them for further study. Of course, illustrations of all of them could be found in Mejuffrouw van Ooosterwijck's numerous folios of botanical engravings, but she believed that a painter could not truly know a plant until she had seen it in all its changing colors, felt the various, changing textures on all its parts. A simple goldenrod, for instance: a day after it had been picked, the blooms were already a slightly different yellow. Drying made the fine down on the stem sharper, more defined.

Jacobus knew the whys of such changes, and so curious was I to understand them that I overcame my natural shyness and my awe of his great intelligence to beg him explain them.

Ten years older than I, he spoke to me as an equal, never seeming to tire of my questions. Indeed, he often shared with me his keen anticipation for the upcoming expedition to the West Indies, paging through folios filled with exotic flowers he would soon see, tracing their shapes lightly with his fingertip, as if their painted petals were real and he must take care not to bruise them. When he did so, his face took on a dreamy expression, spots of color appeared on his pale cheeks, and I thought he must be imagining himself in that faraway place, those very flowers alive and abundant all around him.

But what I liked best about him was the way he discovered something extraordinary in the most homely of plants. Holding my drying goldenrod to his nose, he breathed in the scent; then smiled, and held it to mine.

"Do you smell it?" he asked. "Anise?"

It did smell faintly of anise, and I breathed in that foreign scent, wondering if some exotic flower he would find in the Indies might have a surprisingly familiar scent, one that might remind him of afternoons spent with me in Delft.

Autumn came and deepened, as it must. Leaves flared up in color, dying. Father prepared to travel to Amsterdam to attend to Grandmother's interests there before winter set in; and to my great surprise, he decided that I should accompany him. It was necessary to my education as a painter, he told Grandmother. It was time I saw some of the many Italian works available for viewing in that city.

Upon hearing the news, Maria prevailed upon Grandmother to bid Father take her instead. But he was firm in his intent; and I could not help but feel some satisfaction in the bitterness with which my sister must accept that I would be the first of us to see the world beyond our little town of Delft.

We would travel by *trekschuiten*, a horse-drawn barge, leaving well before dawn, for it would be a full day's journey. The night before, I barely slept. Once, when I did doze off, I dreamed myself at the head of a canal boat, sailing into the open sea—and, glancing toward the sound of wings fluttering, I saw Mijnheer Fabritius's goldfinch flying along beside me.

I drew back the bed curtain at the first sound of Tanneke in the kitchen, and rose to meet the day. She wrapped bread and cheese for Father and me, sustenance for our journey, and bade us bundle up warmly to ward off the pleurisy that would surely be a menace in the humidity of the canal boat.

Braiding my hair, she leaned close and whispered, "Take care if you should see any person with a blemished face, Carelina—for the red marks you see may be the trace of the devil's claw!"

But I was not afraid. Walking through our town with Father that chilly morning, I thought only of the marvels I should soon see and of the summer morning so long ago, when I followed him to the house where he would paint his *View of Delft*. It was still there, its windows dark. And there were women on the quay, as there had been that other morning, waiting for the fishermen to come in with the morning catch. Soon, the sun would rise and the town would emerge, blue and red and gold, beneath it. But by then, Father and I would be well gone.

We boarded and found a bench that, once daylight came, would allow us to view the countryside as we glided by. But when the bell rang and the boatman urged the horses forward, there was still just the flickering of lanterns at quayside, which soon dissolved into complete darkness as we left the town behind us. I slept then, leaning against Father's shoulder.

I awoke to flat, gold and green meadows as far as I could see; and, now and then, the reddish brown smudge of a town on the horizon, its towers and rooftops outlined low beneath the vast blue sky. The air was cool, but the sunshine filtering down through the canopy of linden trees lining the waterway warmed me. Bright leaves drifted down, gathering on the deck and benches or settling on the surface of the water, where they were caught, swirling, in our wake—gentle re-minders that winter was on the way. But I did not shiver at the thought; rather, I imagined how cozy it must be to visit with Mejuffrouw van Oosterwijck and Geertje at that time of year, sur-rounded by painted flowers. Suddenly, vividly, I remembered the warmth of a porcelain teacup in my hand, the way I breathed in the fragrant vapor as I drank. Geertje's cakes, sprinkled with sugar. And I was filled with gratitude, for at that moment I could imagine nothing better than to be having this adventure with Father and such dear friends waiting with anticipation to hear the stories I should tell about it upon my return.

We took on more passengers at The Hague, important-looking men in black coats who settled into the salon of the boat, spectacles perched on their noses, and bent, scribbling, over sheaves of documents. Indeed, we picked up passengers at each stop, and by the time we approached Amsterdam, near dusk, the boat was full to bursting with every sort of person, many of whom engaged with one another in spirited conversation to pass the time. Some sang, using song-books the friendly boatman had provided. But Father and I rode quietly, he smoking his pipe, perhaps painting inside his head, and I watching, listening, breathing in the new, wider world that I had waited so long to enter.

Once in Amsterdam, we made our way by the light of Father's lantern to Mijnheer de Hoogh's home in the Koninjenstraat. A fellow guildsman and dear friend of Father's from his days as a young painter in Delft, Mijnheer de Hoogh had taken up residence in Amsterdam some years ago, after the death of his wife, and Father was always glad for the opportunity to see him. The two embraced on the doorstep, and Mijnheer de Hoogh bade us come in and warm ourselves near the fire while he went to the kitchen to fetch the meal his maid had kindly left for us: rich, warm pea and prune soup, flavored with ginger, and a beautiful Delft plate piled high with bread, cheese, and herring. We ate gratefully, and then, tucked into a cozy cupboard bed, I drifted off to sleep to the sound of the two friends talking about a simpler time, when Fabritius was still with them, when they were all three young and life a blank canvas, full of promise.

Of the next few days in Amsterdam, I remember the press of traffic on the narrow streets: carriages and sledges, people hurrying by. The call of merchants, horses braying. The cry of gulls circling the harbor. I remember tall, elegant houses mirrored in the canals, the massive Town Hall with its dome and bell turret. And the way the air vibrated with what must have been a thousand bells.

I remember, too, the Carpaccio shown me by Father's friend, a dealer in Italian paintings. It was a view of Venice as opposite of Father's *View of Delft* as a painting of a town could be—yet it held me as Father's painting had. So full of life! Ladies and gentlemen dressed in silk and velvet lounged on parapets draped with Turkish rugs, gathered on bridges that arched over canals teeming with gondolas and barges piled high with goods. It seemed to me that I could hear the splash of the gondoliers' poles in the water, smell the damp breeze coming in from the sea.

Another world. Perhaps listening to Jacobus speak of his upcoming expedition had made me begin to believe that, in time, I must leave the world I knew, my Father's world, if I were to find happiness, and that is why I remember the painting so vividly. Perhaps it is because the image of the painting is inextricably bound to the memory of the news Father gave me on the day I saw it.

We were on our return journey, nearing home, when he tipped my face up toward him with his hand and said, "Carelina, there is something I must speak to you about."

I smiled, for I believed he meant to tell me that, at last, he would resume teaching me, this time in earnest. Why would he have taken me to see the great works of art that had influenced him in his youth, if not as a prelude to beginning the next phase of my education?

"*Dochterken*," he began.

And I felt the smile fade from my face, because I heard sadness in the tone of his voice, in the endearment he so often used when he must tell me something he knew would disappoint me.

"You cannot know what a great pleasure you are to me," he said.

"What a joy it is to see the world through your eyes. To have you at work beside me."

Tears sprang to my eyes at his words, and when they fell to my cheek, he scooped them away with his blunt finger.

"Carelina, Mejuffrouw van Oosterwijck has developed a great fondness for you in these past months, and she has recently come to me with an offer to apprentice you. I cannot—" He looked away from me for a moment, toward the countryside slowly turning gray with dusk. "My obligations make it impossible to continue to teach you myself, and I—"

"Grandmother," I said bitterly.

He gave a small shrug. "Obligations to Grandmother, yes. They take a great deal of my time, and will take more. But it is your mother, too, and the little ones who need my attention. And Carelina, Mejuffrouw van Oosterwijck has resources to help you that I would never have, even if I should formally apprentice you myself. I should be remiss if I did not give your education over to her care. You understand this," he said. "And you are fond of Mejuffrouw van Oosterwijck, I know. You have learned a great deal from her already. In time, you will be grateful for what must be."

I did understand. I saw that in Father's decision to apprentice me to Mejuffrow van Oosterwyck, he meant to save me from the nearly certain fate of an odd, plain daughter in a family with no little or no dowry to offer a prospective husband. I saw that, but for this intervention in Grandmother Thins's plan for me, I should have lived to serve my mother and sisters all my days: dutiful daughter, doting maiden aunt.

And it was true that I was fond of Mejuffrouw van Oosterwijyck, and Geertje too. That I had learned from them already, blossomed in their approval of me. Father was right to let me go. In the part of

me that knew this, a kind of singing rose up; but it was balanced by
sorrow for the loss of light-drenched mornings in the painting room
with my father.

"*The Art of Painting*!" Mijnheer van Hoogstraaten pronounced,
"Fabritius himself would have deemed it a wonder!"

He recited Arnold Bon's poem that had recently been published
in Van Bleyswyck's *Beschyrvinge der Stadt Delft*:

> *Thus died this Phoenix when he was thirty years of age,*
> *In the midst and in the best of his powers.*
> *But happily there rose from his fire*
> *Vermeer, who master-like, was able to emulate him.*

He raised the glass of ale that Jutte had just poured for him. The
painting, framed now, hung on the wall at Mechelen, where we had
come to celebrate its completion.

The tavern was full. There were many fellow painters from the
guild, as well as Mijnheer de Hoogh and Mijnheer Metsu from
Amsterdam and Mijnheer Dou from Leiden. Mijnheer de Cocq from
Papists' Corner was in attendance; so were Mijnheer van Leeuwen-
hoek and Mijnheer van Ruijven, with Magdalena. Mejuffrouw van
Oosterwijck and Geertje, too.

Mijnheer van Ruijven had offered his carriage so that Mother
might be with us. Father had carried her inside and settled her into
the comfortable chair that Grandma Digna had provided. Now he
stood beside her, receiving congratulations from the guests. Mother
had not been out since the death of the stillborn child, and it lightened my heart to see her away from Grandmother Thins's hovering
presence. I was glad that Grandmother had chosen to remain at

home, brooding over Father's refusal to sell the painting to Mijnheer van Ruijven, glad it was just our own family here to celebrate Father's accomplishment. Cornelia had insisted on bringing the little ones, too, and she had bathed them, dressed them in their best clothes, and instructed them how to behave properly. Even the unruly Johannes, four now, had taken her lessons to heart, and conducted himself like a little man, delighting Father's colleagues with his firm handshake.

My own delight I kept to myself, for I knew it to be unworthy. I had watched Maria preen for the occasion all morning, assuming she would be the center of attention; now I watched her wilt like a flower. I watched her face, so beautiful on the canvas, take on a bored, sullen expression as Mijnheer van Hoogstraaten held forth on the painting's many virtues.

"The figure," he called her. "The model. Clio. The muse." Never "Maria."

"The yellow book she holds!" He placed his hand upon his heart. "And her delicate fingers on the trumpet! See how the laurel leaves in her crown are repeated in the tapestry and again, beneath the painter's brush. The way her downcast eyes direct you to the mask on the table, which directs you across the folio to the painter, whose gaze carries you across the known world, back to her face. Ah, that face!"

Maria glanced up, suddenly attentive.

"Made of light and shadows," Mijnheer van Hoogstraaten went on. "Truly, it is a miracle of a face. Yet what the painter sees, what consumes him in this caught moment is the laurel wreath on her head, an allegorical prop. His hand on his canvas covers the place where the face will be. Indeed, this hand proclaims its own supremacy. From it will come Clio's face. The painter's heart, his world."

He sat down, flushed with the expression of such heady emotion; and the dejected expression on Maria's face made me feel sorry for

149

her, ashamed of the pleasure I had felt to see her ignored. Perhaps Mejuffrouw van Oosterwijck had been watching her, too, for she made her way to the table where Maria sat. I could not hear what she said, but I saw Maria's face brighten at the attention. I supposed Mejuffrouw van Oosterwijck had told her what she was hoping to hear. That she was beautiful, that it was an honor to have been chosen as Father's model. I contemplated this and found I did not mind. Secure in the knowledge her friendship and affection, I listened to talk about *The Art of Painting* swirl around me.

"The tapestry, drawn back, surely a reference to the ancient competition between Zeuxix and Parrhasius to see which could paint the most realistic painting."

"The painter's red stockings!"

"The chair in the foreground, as if placed there so the viewer might enter and take a seat."

"And the light! How it dazzles. How it defines everything, even the map, with its meticulously rendered folds and faults."

"That long vertical cracquelature there," someone mused. "See how it falls just short of the painter's hat. It passes through Breda, divides the north and south provinces. Clearly, it is meant to allude to our history. A happier time . . ."

"Yes! And the chandelier with the Hapsburg eagle, the painter's doublet seem an echo of that sentiment."

"Ha!" A third voice spoke. "That same line leads you right into the blackness of the painter's hat—into his head, if you will, where he is conceiving the painting on the canvas."

"It is a map," Mijnheer van Hoogstraaten said. "That's all. Why must it mean something more? Pleasure enough in the painter's challenge to render it—and the other objects, as well. This is a painting about the pleasure of painting. Is it not so, Jan?"

Father smiled enigmatically. It was the same smile he had given Grandmother Thins when he told her he would not sell *The Art of Painting* at any price. The unseen smile that I knew the painter in the painting smiled, brush poised to create the ordered world around him.

✛✛✛✛✛✛✛✛✛✛✛✛✛✛✛✛✛✛✛✛✛✛✛✛✛✛✛✛✛

# EPILOGUE

✛✛✛✛✛✛✛✛✛✛✛✛✛✛✛✛✛✛✛✛✛✛✛✛✛✛✛✛✛

H, THE gavel falls, interrupting my reverie, and Father's *View of Delft* goes for 200 guilders. Our mother, *A Young Lady Weighing Gold*, brings 155; Tanneke, *A Maid Pouring Out Milk*, 175. In all, Mijnheer van Ruijven's collection of Father's paintings brings 1,500 guilders, a respectable enough amount. But I cannot help thinking, those buying them do not truly *see*. They cannot fathom what these paintings cost in terms of our own human hearts.

*The Art of Painting* is not among them. Mijnheer van Ruiven had greatly desired it; but Father held firm against Grandmother Thins's protestations and would not sell it at any price. Indeed, despite the most dire financial circumstances, he managed to keep the painting until the end of his life. Afterward, Mother lowered herself to the most cunning deceptions in the hope that she might save turning it over to his creditors. Alas, in time, the painting was given up to them, and soon disappeared. Where it is now, I do not know. And, in truth, I am grateful not to see it among the others today.

Nor *Allegory of Faith*, the last painting Father made. Commissioned by the Jesuits, this work defeated him and made him old before his time. Then and now, I could not bear to look at it: our mother, ecstatic against the backdrop of the crucified Christ, and all around her, the accoutrements of faith. He had made the painting not long after our Grandma Digna's death; and, even all these years

155

later, the simple thought of it fills me with dread. I remember the knock on the door near bedtime, the sight of Tanneke ushering in our Uncle Antony, hat in hand, on the night he came to fetch Father so that he might be with his dear mother at the end. I remember grabbing my cloak and following the men out into the darkness, arriving, breathless, to find the predicant reciting prayers for the dying.

I stood back, my hands hidden beneath my cloak so that I might secretly slip the cool beads of my rosary through my fingers. I feared for my grandmother's soul, prayed that at the sight of Father she might send the predicant away and come, finally, to the true faith. But it was not to be.

Indeed, there on her deathbed, Grandma Digna whispered to Father her belief that his salvation was a matter of grace. The Lord knew his goodness. He would forgive Father his conversion, and she would rest in peace with the knowledge that, in time, he would join her and his beloved father in Heaven. She fell silent then, and I waited to hear the dark flapping of Satan's wings; but there was only Grandma's rasping breath. My breath, the predicant's, Aunt Gertruy's.

And my father's. He did not speak, just knelt before his mother like a supplicant. She smiled at him, the smile of an angel. She took his hand and bade him lean forward so that she could put it to her lips. So that his face would dominate her ebbing vision.

"My Johannes," she said. "My boy."

She closed her eyes then, drew her last breath.

Father sat there beside her for a long while, his head in his hands, quietly weeping. When the room emptied, where Aunt Gertruy and the predicant went, I do not know. Nor do I know how long it was before Father pulled the bed sheet over Grandma Digna's face and closed the velvet bedcurtains. I remember only walking with him through the dark streets, toward home.

It was a cold night. February. Snow on the ground, an occasional skater gliding past, bent low for speed, his hands tucked behind his back. It must have been near ten o'clock, for I remember the roll of the drum and the sound of footsteps as the guard gathered to form its night patrol. Inside the houses, people were banking their fires, kneeling for their evening prayers. We walked slowly, Father and I, the light from his torch casting shadows that leapt like spirits on the cobblestones before us.

I shivered, not only from the cold. I could not help fearing for Grandma Digna's soul; but I did not share my concern with Father, for I knew he would say, simply, *God knows who is good*. It was what he said in response to almost any question of faith that I had ever asked him, and the words had always been a comfort. Now it struck me that the words Grandma Digna had spoken to Father from her deathbed expressed the same belief. But how could that be?

Father was Catholic. His love for our mother had brought him to the true faith; and to receive it, he had set aside the Calvinist beliefs of his youth. It would be a sin for him to believe, as Grandma did, that the salvation of one's soul was a simple matter of grace, for it went against the most fundamental Catholic belief that salvation must be earned through goodness and faith. The Catholic faith, of course—though quite suddenly it occurred to me that I had never actually heard Father say that there was just one way to believe. Oddly, I saw, in my mind's eye, the repeated image of the church tower I had once seen through the dragonfly's eye on Mijnheer van Leeuwenhoek's lens.

"What is real?" he had asked me.

I could not answer his question then, or on the night of Grandma Digna's death. Indeed, I still cannot answer it. With each passing year, the world becomes more rather than less a conundrum to me, each of us viewing it as we do through our own set of eyes that splinter what we see with feeling and memory.

In any case, it was this moment, not—as Grandmother Thins believed—my association with Mejuffrouw van Oosterwijck, that caused my little sphere of existence to crack open and admit the winds of change. I was haunted by the image of myself clutching my rosary beads, so fearful of the wrath of our Lord that I could not make myself move toward the circle of light where my dear grandma lay. Of all the children, she had loved me best. I knew this, for she had told me so, and no vision of heaven or hell could balance the shame and sorrow I felt remembering that, at the moment of her death, I had not even tried to bring her comfort.

It was during this time that my father painted me. Perhaps he understood my need for stillness, perhaps he knew how his hands arranging me, his eyes upon me gave me presence and weight. Perhaps the need was his own and I was but a play of light and color to distract him from his sadness. What matters, what I know is that the painting of me was the last one made purely of love. I know, too, that holding me there before him for a time was the only way he knew to give me help. For he had changed after our grandmother's death. He became like a figure in the last paintings he made: set back into the interior, distant and abstract.

Indeed, his own death came but four years after hers. He left our poor mother bereft, so encumbered with debt that when Delft's *Camer van Charitate* came for the traditional death donation, "*niet to halen*" must be recorded in their book—nothing to get. He was buried in Grandmother Thins's vault in the Oude Kerk, the tiny coffin of yet another lost child resting upon him, and our mother was forever afterwards dependent upon Grandmother for her sustenance and that of her living children.

This I could not bear; and so it was I turned away from my family completely and went to live in Mejuffouw Van Oosterwijck's house. But the solace she gave me was not, as Grandmother Thins imagined, religious in nature. It was in no way an effort on her part to convert me to her faith. Indeed, in all those years we never spoke of faith at all. We spoke of flowers.

Even in winter, her house was full of them, brought by barge several times a week from the vast greenhouses near Haarlem, and on those days when my spirits were at their lowest ebb she would pluck a single bloom from a bouquet and bid me look at it. A tulip, a carnation, a snapdragon, a rose. She need not tell me that it did not matter what the flower was, only that I look hard enough to lose myself in the curve of its petals, in some pattern of tiny blossoms thrusting up from its stem. She need not tell me of her sorrow for the loss of my father, either. I knew it from her expression, from the way she sat patiently beside me. I would look and look and, in time, the world dissolved. My burden lightened. Then, quietly, she would speak to me.

"See how the petals grow in twos," she might say. "But no two exactly alike, no two with exactly the same relation to each other."

Or, "That brown spot. Don't you find it interesting?"

And I did. Whereas my father had been infinitely fascinated by the effect of light on changing objects, I had learned to love painting flowers for the way they themselves changed. Father had lived praying the light would return in a certain way, so that it might again illuminate an object he was bound to capture; but a flower was dying even as I painted it. Its changes were forever.

Ah, these memories: it was another time. And best kept behind me.

Indeed, it is the greatest of coincidences that I am here in Amsterdam on the day of this sale at all; for I have lived many years now in the West Indies with my dear husband and will return soon, when his series of lectures at the University of Leiden is through. It is always warm there, and so wet in places that steam rises up from the forest floors and collects, drinkable, in the cup-like blossoms of trees. There are arid places, too, with thorny scrub and succulents growing up through the rock from which the land was formed. And the sea, with its own rich life within. We travel these lands, Jacobus and I. He names the marvelous plants we discover, and I paint them so that he may keep a record of his work. I paint the native women we have come to know, as well, standing serenely in their own light, the simple accoutrements of their lives arranged around them.

It is a good life that I have with my husband, a quiet life. At times, luminous, and it is in those luminous moments when my dear father comes to me, and I may receive his spirit with complete, unmitigated joy.

# AUTHOR'S NOTE

*Vermeer's Daughter* is entirely a work of fiction, based on the life of the seventeenth-century Dutch painter, Johannes Vermeer. Delft town records show that Vermeer was born and baptized a Protestant in 1632, and that his parents, Reynier Janszoon and Digna Baltens, were the proprietors of a tavern, Mechelen, on Great Markt Square. There are some speculations, but no certainty about who his teachers were, though it is generally thought that he was influenced as a young man by the painter, Carel Fabritius, a former apprentice of Rembrandt's who resided in Delft for several years before his death in a powder explosion there in 1654. Vermeer married Catharina Bolnes at the Catholic church in Schipluy in 1653, and they lived most of their married life with Catharina's mother, Maria Thins. The births of eleven children are recorded; some historians believe that they may have had as many as fifteen. The main character of this book, Vermeer's daughter Carelina, is a fictional daughter, her birthdate placed between the known birthdates of two of Vermeer's real daughters, Maria and Elisabeth. As many of Vermeer's painting are undated, I have taken the liberty of dating them to suit the structure of the story.

Vermeer was an active, well-respected painter during his lifetime, serving several terms as Head Man of the St. Luke's Guild in Delft; however, after his death, he was more or less forgotten until the late nineteenth century. No personal or historical narrative of his life is known to exist, and so art historians have had to approximate an outline of his life based on archival documents and on the observation of his small existing oeuvre of thirty-four paintings. The most definitive of these historical works is *Vermeer and His Milieu: A Web of Social History*, by John Michael Montias. This book, as well as books of art history and criticism by Arthur Wheelock, Svetlana Alpers, Lawrence Gowing, Edward Snow, and Albert Blankert, have provided much of the factual and critical information about Vermeer's life and work for this novel. Also invaluable were Simon Schama's *An Embarrassment of Riches: An Interpretation of Dutch Culture in the Golden Age*, Wayne E. Franits's *Paragons of Virtue: Women and Domesticity in Seventeenth Century Dutch Art*, Zbigniew Herbert's *Still Life With a Bridle*, and Paul Zumthor's *Daily Life in Rembrandt's Time*.